SAPPHIC SIZZLE

AN EROTIC ROMANCE ANTHOLOGY

Sapphic Sizzle: An Erotic Romance Anthology

PUBLISHED BY:
Jug Run Press, USA

Copyright © 2022 Anne Hagan, Johana Gavez, Kitty McIntosh, Kim Hartfield, Adrian J. Smith, Elle Armstrong, LL Shelton, Raven J. Spencer, KC Luck, and Alyson Tong

Publication Date: August 1st, 2022

Paperback ISBN: 978-1-950828-13-5

eBook ISBN: 978-1-950828-14-2

TABLE OF CONTENTS

BEFORE DANA

ANNE HAGAN

Before Dana, long before Dana, Mel knew she was different. It would take her years to act on her desire for close female contact. When she did? Fire!

A sexy prequel to the Morelville Mysteries series starring Sheriff Melissa 'Mel' Crane.

I played softball in high school. It was a small country school with only twelve girls on the team. It's not bragging for me to say I was pretty good–got a couple of college scholarship offers–but my team was not. We never even got into the play-offs until my senior year and only then because my twin sister, Kris, and I carried the team on our backs. We didn't get far.

One girl on the team, Lori, seemed different from all the others. There was something about her that drew me to her. I was interested. Intrigued. Infatuated. I just didn't know to call it any of those things then. We gravitated toward each other, became friends. She was a decent ball player, not great, but she was sweet and funny and nice. My folks had her out on the farm a few times. Dad loved her, found her quite charming.

I took a sports scholarship and went off to school for the 1992 fall semester. She went to college on a music scholarship - drums - a couple states away.

College didn't work out for me. With only a semester under my belt, I figured out the academic life was not what I wanted and gave up my scholarship. It seemed to work just fine for Lori, though.

I went on to the peace officers' training academy after a handful of months knocking around on the farm. If Lori ever came back to the county for visits while she was in college, it's lost on me.

1998

The early November rain was falling steadily when I stepped out of my cruiser. *Cold!* I shivered against it as it hit my cap and rolled down my cheeks. I'd learned to hate the rain as a rookie riding along with a training officer. Now on my own, it wasn't any better. There's nothing worse to a deputy than something stupid happening that means them having to get out of their vehicle in the pouring rain. For a speeder, it's a guaranteed ticket.

The park closed at dusk. An employee called about an occupied vehicle in an otherwise deserted lot he passed as he was leaving the back side of the park, the occupants paying him no mind. He didn't want to get involved. That's where I came in.

As I approached the lone car on foot, I knew what I was dealing with; a couple of young lovers who were oblivious to the time and everything else going on around them. The fogged over windows were the only clue I needed.

If the bouncing around that appeared to be going on inside was any sign, they hadn't heard me pull up. I tried clearing my throat close to the rear passenger window. They didn't hear me. I called out, "Police! Cease and desist. The park is closed, and you need to move along." Nothing. The damn rain was coming down even harder and drowning me out.

I tapped on the window. A woman inside shouted out, but the tone of the 'OH GOD,' I heard told me she probably wasn't talking to me.

I tried the back door handle. Locked. The front passenger side door handle worked just fine, though.

I don't know if it was the whoosh of rain and cold air entering the vehicle or me sticking my head inside that scared the two occupants more. What I do remember about that night is the instant reaction in my loins and the hardening of my nipples even with a bra, protective vest, uniform shirt, and raincoat on, when I realized the lovers were both women. Beautiful, very naked women.

The scent. As much as I remember those women, I remember the scent in that car. It was intoxicating to me in a way no liquor ever had been.

I let them get dressed and sent them on their way. I never even got their names, not that night, anyway. That night was my awakening. That was the night I finally knew for sure.

Summer 2001

My dad is a music fan. All kinds, especially anything he can dance to. He enjoyed taking us to local concerts, hoedowns, square dances and just about any other get together with music while we were growing up. If it was cheap or free and it wasn't keeping us out too much past bedtime on a school night–even as seniors–we were there. His love of music rubbed off on me.

I split my off time when I'm not helping at the farm between ball games and concerts. There's t-ball, little league, high school baseball and softball, college ball at a nearby liberal arts school, you name it. The concerts? They're as eclectic for me as they are for my dad.

My sister mentioned to me one Thursday that I should go with her to the Boar's Head on Saturday night, since I was off for a change. She told me an old friend I might want to see was playing with a band that was coming through Zanesville. I didn't even ask who. I figured, why not? I mean, why question it? It was music and I'm always up for that when I'm not working.

———

I remember the bar was getting crowded. Smoky. I hated that. Still do. At least it was a decent night out, and the doors were all open. The ceiling fans moved some air through. Still, there was a haze about the stage as some roadies set up equipment.

My sister despised being late. Even more than Kris hated to be late, she hated to not have her pick of seats. So, there we were, front and center, just off the dance floor across from the tiny stage, the bar filling up for a set that wouldn't start for at least another hour.

I ordered food and the only beer I'd allow myself to have all night and settled in to wait. I was used to hurry up and wait. First Dad, then the academy, then long nights in a patrol car with nothing much happening in a rural county, and now Kris.

Two men pushed carts of speakers in through a door near the stage, then a woman in a short skirt and a plaid shirt knotted at the waist stepped through the door. She looked at the stage and then out at the room, sizing things up. She looked familiar, but I couldn't figure out why.

I glanced at my sister for a clue. "Is that who we're here to see?"

"Lori? Yes."

Lori. How could I not have recognized her?

Kris half stood and waved to get her attention.

Lori came right over. Kris was standing by then and pulled her into a quick hug.

Hey, she was my friend, not yours. I stood too. I felt like I was 17 again. She looked as good to me as an adult woman as she had as a teenager. All my old feelings came rushing back.

We're hugging. She's hugging me. She felt amazing. I did my best to control myself and not crush her to me. At least, I think I did.

"Hey there," she said to me. "So nice to see you." She ran a hand through my hair, sending electricity down my spine. "Sorry to be so forward, but it looks so good short like that. And it's so thick!"

Lori turned back to Kris for a moment. "I see you still keep yours long." She asked me, "Did you cut yours so people could finally tell you two apart?"

"No, actually, I did it for my job. Makes it easier."

"What are you doing now, Melissa?"

"Mel, please. Everyone just calls me Mel now. Well, except our mom."

Kris chimed in with, "She won't have it. Says Mel is bastardizing a perfectly good name."

"Mel suits you and your look," Lori said, "but you still didn't answer my question. What have you been up to since college? I'm so sorry we lost touch..."

I remember shrugging, searching for words that I didn't think would sound dumb. I pulled out a chair for her and plunged in while she took a seat. "I left college and went to the Ohio Peace Officer's Training Academy. Now, I'm a deputy sheriff here in the county."

Lori arched an eyebrow. "Impressive, and it fits. If I know you, you'll be the county Sheriff one day."

I shook my head at the time. "I have no desire *ever* to do that." If I had only known then what I know now.

"What about you, Kris?"

"Me? I have an infant son, Cole, and I'm working part time

at the gas station in our village. Still helping out on the farm, too."

"A baby? Oh, but you look so good!"

Kris preened. She always did at compliments, even when she fished for them.

"Either of you still play ball?"

"Tournaments only," I answered.

"And?" my sister prompted.

I gave her a look. She ignored it.

"Mel is the high school coach."

"Really now? That's great!"

"Kris is being modest." She wasn't. She just wanted me to brag on her, too. "She's an assistant coach on the team and runs all the pitchers and catchers training sessions." I didn't let Kris make it all about her. "What about you? What have you been up to? Last time I saw you, you were headed off to school on a band scholarship and you were going to study veterinary medicine."

Lori spread her hands. "My plans changed too. College was very freeing, shall we say? I did get a degree in music though, not in medicine. I played drums in the marching band for four years and spent a lot of time composing. I learned guitar, keyboards; you name it. Now I'm touring with these guys, small time stuff mostly, but we just got booked to open for Lee Ann Womack's tour while she swings through the eastern states."

"That's pretty cool," Kris said.

"We're excited. We cut a demo that's making the rounds. That's how she found us. And I'm working on a solo album."

"Of guitar music?" I asked.

"Singing and lead guitar. A little drumming, too. The drums are my first love...in music, that is."

"Lori," a roadie called out. "Sound check?"

Lori stood. "Duty calls. Can we all catch up some more later?"

I nodded quickly. "I'd like that."

Kris was a party-pooper. "I've got to get home to the little one after your first set. Sorry."

"I'll have to run her since we came together," I said. "How long are you in town?"

Lori offered, "I can run you home later, Mel. I've got my car since we're in the area for a break for a few days before we head toward Louisville to meet up with Lee Ann. Our keyboard player is from Columbus. This area is a good place for us all to take a breather for a couple of days."

I looked at Kris. "Do you mind?"

"I do, because I want to hang out too, but Mom has Cole and I promised not to be out too late." She sighed and gave in. "Oh well. Have fun." She didn't mean it. I could always tell when Kris was miffed. I didn't care.

"Lori, we're ready for you," the roadie called out.

"Coming." She sketched a wave and walked away.

"You're incredible," I said, and I meant it. "I never heard you sing before."

She gave me a look. "I was in the choir in high school."

"And the band, and you played ball."

"Don't forget the yearbook staff!"

"You were just an all-around goody-two-shoes."

Lori snorted. "Hardly."

"I stayed far away from the choir. I love music, but I can't carry a tune in a bucket."

"You were in the marching band *and* the concert band. You played those crazy horns."

"Freshman and sophomore years. French horn freshman year and the euphonium sophomore year. I hated that one. That was for my dad. He played it when he was in high school and he thought I'd be good at it."

"You were."

I rolled my eyes and she called me out on it. "You haven't changed, I see. I feel like we're back in high school."

I couldn't keep the goofy grin off my face. "So do I."

Lori put her coffee cup down and laid a hand on mine. "Do you want to get out of here?"

I wasn't ready to go home, but I figured she must be tired. "Sure. I live with Kris in Morelville. I'm sorry it's going to be out of your way."

"While I think it's great that you two are still close enough and tolerant enough of each other to live together, but that wasn't quite what I had in mind."

"Oh...uh, okay."

"You hungry?" she asked me.

"Not really. I ate while you were doing your sound check, but if you are, I'll keep you company."

"No. I'm not."

"Pardon?"

She grinned. "You're so formal. I meant, I'm not hungry. I just wanted to make sure you were good to go." She rose and tossed her head in the direction of the door beside the stage. "I'm parked in back."

Being inside the Holiday Inn Express in Zanesville was an unfamiliar experience for me. A reputable place. I'd never taken a patrol call there. "I hear this place has a nice indoor pool," I said, attempting small talk.

"I wouldn't know," Lori said. "I don't swim much. When we have the money, we try to stay in this chain. They have the best beds; better than the ones on the tour bus by miles."

I swallowed involuntarily.

She headed right for the elevator.

"Are we going to your room?"

"Is that okay?"

"Sure. Yeah. It's fine."

Lori gave me a long look in the elevator before saying, "Can I ask you something?"

The doors slid open on the second floor, and I waved her out ahead of me. "Sure."

She looked back over her shoulder at me. "You seem nervous. Why?"

"I'm not nervous." I dug at the collar of my shirt.

She shook her head and grinned at me as she stepped off. "Relax. It's just us. Oh, and...that wasn't the question."

"What's the question?" I asked back as I followed her down the hall.

She stopped at room 226 and waved a card over the door lock.

Taking me by the hand, she pulled me inside and closed the door. "We wouldn't want anyone who might recognize you gossiping about one of Muskingum County's finest."

"There was no one in the hall."

"Mel."

"Hmm?"

"Are you gay?"

I had figured that was what was coming. I was inexperienced, but not entirely naïve. I knew flirting when I saw it. I'd seen Kris practice it on men many times. Still, I wasn't exactly prepared with an answer. "Yes. At least, I think so."

She tugged me further into the room, kicking off her shoes

as she went. We passed a rather large bed I figured must be king sized, skirted a coffee table, and landed on a small couch that barely held the two of us.

She told me, "I'm not trying to get you into bed. That's not why I brought you here." She got up and walked to a mini-fridge. I tried not to feel disappointed or to stare.

She grabbed two bottles of water and held one up.

I nodded.

"Bars tear me up. All that smoke is so hard on the vocal cords." She cracked her bottle open and set it on the table.

"But you're not going to drink it?"

"Not yet. Too cold. That's also bad for the vocal cords. You go ahead though."

I was sweating. I wanted the drink. I needed the drink. I opened mine, took a swig, then asked, "So why are we here?"

She was ready. "No cigarette smoke and it's a lot more private for conversation." She sat back down with her legs tucked up underneath her. I missed them.

"So," I began, mad at my voice for shaking, "you said you weren't trying to get me into bed. Does that mean that...that you're—"

Lori nodded, putting me out of my misery. "Yes. I knew in high school I preferred girls over boys." She winked at me. "Why do you think I spent all of my time with you?"

I capped my water and put it down with a shaking hand before I spilled it. "I just thought we were best friends."

"We were. Is that all you thought? Did you think about anything else?"

I closed my eyes, going back to those days, briefly reliving certain special moments. "You. I thought about you all the time," I admitted.

"Why do you suppose that was?"

"I didn't know back then, Lori. Honestly, I didn't."

"Oh, I believe you. You can barely acknowledge it now. So, tell me, when did you figure it all out?"

I told her about that night in the state park, seeing those women.

She threw her head back and laughed. Her long hair trailed along the back of the couch.

"It wasn't funny at the time." I couldn't help myself though, and I started laughing with her.

She reached out a hand and laid it on my shoulder. "Look at me."

I did as I was told.

"Have you ever been with a woman?"

"No. Not exactly."

"Define, not exactly, officer."

"Deputy."

"You're avoiding the question."

I swallowed. "No."

"No, what?"

"No; I've never been with a woman. Never even kissed one."

"Ever been on a date with one?"

"Does tonight count?"

"No."

"Then, no." I turned the tables. "Enough about my failings. Tell me about you."

She shook her head but left her hand in place. I could feel the warmth of it burning through my shirt. "There's not a lot to tell. We lived in a rural county, Mel. I figured it all out in high school but knew I couldn't ever act on it there, do what I so desperately wanted to do."

"What was that?" I was half scared of what her answer might be.

"Talk to you. Tell you." She paused for several beats. "Kiss you."

I let that sink in for a minute. "We lost touch."

Lori nodded. "I heard from my mom that you quit school, went back to the farm. College was...eye opening for me. I couldn't come back here and give up the freedom I found there."

"Yeah. I get that. Honestly, things still haven't changed much here."

"It wasn't all perfect for me either, Mel. I've had my heart broken badly. Twice."

"By women?"

She bobbed her head. "Somehow, I think that's harder to take, but I really have nothing to compare it to."

"I admit, I dated some men. Never got that into them to be that emotional about getting dumped by them."

She leaned back a little and gave me a look. "Hard to believe you got dumped, ever."

"I'm a twin, remember? Guys thought I was like Kris. I'm not. Far from it."

"Is the baby daddy in the picture for her?"

"Nope. Of course not."

"Ah. Explains a lot."

Feeling bolder, I changed the subject again. "So, what's it like being with a woman?"

"Day to day? A lot like being with a guy, I suspect, but with lots more feelings and emotions."

I softly slapped her hand that was on my shoulder. "You know what I meant."

"Sex?"

I swallowed. "Yeah."

She leaned really close and whispered, "Even when it's bad, it's amazing."

I could feel her breath on my face until she moved away a little.

"I can see a question in your eyes," she said.

Summoning every ounce of courage I had, I asked, "Lori, are you seeing anybody?"

She shook her head. "Not a soul." She waved her free hand outward and shrugged. "Life on the road."

"The guys in the band do they...know? Are they—"

"Let's put it this way: two of them are a couple." She pointed a finger at me. "That's between us. We're a country band. The other is married to a lovely woman who travels with us a lot."

"Wow. Okay. What about the roadies?"

She wasn't having it. "What's your real question?"

"I...this is hard."

Lori gave me an in. "Do you want to be with me, Mel?"

All I could do was nod.

To my disappointment, she moved away slightly as far as the tiny couch would let her go. She leaned forward and picked her bottle of water up off the table and took a small sip, holding it in her mouth for a few moments before swallowing.

"You're uncomfortable." I stood. "I should go."

She reached for my hand and tugged me back down. "Not uncomfortable. Unsure. Unsure if you really know what you're getting—"

I leaned toward her. "I know."

Her kiss was soft, tentative at first, and sweet. Sweet, but it set me on fire.

Lori pushed me into a reclining position on the sofa, my back against one end, my feet on the floor. She came up on her knees and positioned herself over my right leg.

My arms encircled her, held her tight. I groaned at the contact. She felt even better than she had earlier in the evening when I'd had to restrain myself in public. I accepted her completely, allowing her to mold her form to mine.

Her tongue probed gently at my lips. I let it in. There was moaning. It was several long seconds later before I realized it was me. Her body, her lips. They felt so good.

The knee resting against my crotch had feelings stirring in me I hadn't felt in a long time. Not since the last night I had pictured those two women in that car and pleasured myself with the images playing out in my mind.

She moved her mouth to my neck. My lips missed her, but my nipples tightened as she moved my shirt collar away and kissed along my collarbone. She pulled back a little and began undoing the buttons of my shirt.

I grinned.

"What?"

"I feel like I should be doing that to you."

"We have all night, Mel."

Kris and what she would think if I never came home briefly passed crossed my mind, but Lori's lips found the base of my neck, and then her tongue started licking lower. Thoughts of anyone else but her had to wait.

We were both shirtless, braless, and still struggling on the tiny couch when Lori suggested we move to the bed.

I didn't want to move away from her and the delicious skin to skin contact that had me reeling, but she was up and away before I could string two words together.

When I got to my feet, I realized I still had my boots on. I had to sit back down to pull them off, breaking the mood, making Lori laugh.

"Sure you don't want your first time to be with your boots on, sexy?"

"Ha, ha. These were for the bar, not for bed."

"You won't be sleeping. Not anytime soon."

I sure hoped not. "Oh, I'm wide awake."

Lori walked me backward to the bed as she undid the button on my Levi's. I sat down when I came in contact with the mattress, but she pushed me to my back then got on top after directing me to shift around.

Her weight felt delicious on me. I held her tight to me as our lips met again.

No longer sweet, her kiss was hot. The heat was so intense, I writhed under her.

Lori slipped a knee between my legs and pressed hard. Every nerve ending in my core thrummed. I could feel my wetness.

She got up on her knees over me and worked my zipper down, then hooked her hands into my waistband and yanked.

I arched up, letting her pull my jeans down. She stood and completely removed the Levis, but left my boxers and her skirt on.

When she was close enough, I reached a hand up the skirt, skimmed her thigh and ran my fingers along the crotch of her panties. They were silky and slick with her wetness. Her shudder told me she was as on edge as I was. I pulled her back down to me.

When I put my hands on her ass, she ground her pelvis into mine. I felt like I was going to explode. Lori wasn't close to letting me finish, though. She licked at both of my nipples, then clasped her lips around one and sucked. It was amazing and torture all in one. I wanted to try it on her.

Bigger and presumably stronger, I tried to roll us over to get the upper hand. Halfway over, she slapped my right buttock hard and commanded, "Be patient. You'll get your turn," then she rolled me back onto my back.

I gave in, letting the sensations she was giving me wash over me. Her attention to my nipples had a direct effect on my clit. It throbbed with ache and need.

Lori took pity on me–maybe I was whining a little–and kissed her way lower, down my stomach, to my core.

I didn't know how her mouth was going to feel on me, but I couldn't wait to find out. She shocked me by raising up a little, inching down my boxers, and tracing my folds with two fingers instead. I shuddered. I couldn't help it.

She stroked a single finger upward, finishing with a light graze of my clit. "You're so wet."

"You are too."

"Honey, I've been wet since I walked into that bar and saw you."

"No..."

She nodded. "Yes." She took one of my hands and guided it inside her panties. "Just a quick feel. Your turn will come after I make you crazy."

What I could feel was liquid heat. Too soon, she pulled my hand out and licked my fingers, tasting herself on them. I put them to my nose and inhaled. The scent of her desire was still pungent.

"Lay back," Lori whispered. "Enjoy. I'm going to show you how a woman makes love to a woman."

"Is there a test later?"

"Oh yes. Hands on."

To my surprise, Lori slowed our pace. She lay alongside of me rather than resuming her position of control on top of me.

We kissed. Long. Slow. So hot.

She ran a hand up and down my side, shoulder to boxers, then she lavished attention on my breasts and nipples. I was quickly learning how they could be so sensitive, such centers of pure pleasure.

As she held me up on my side and tongued one nipple, she moved her wandering hand around me and massaged my lower back, buttocks, and the back of my thigh. I loved being close to her, loved her touch.

Several minutes of blissful torture later, Lori kept her mouth on a nipple, but stopped caressing me. Her hand found its way between my legs. I parted them at her nudge, and she took control of my core.

As she stroked my folds, then went deeper into my wetness, I moaned. It felt so good. She stroked up and down and circled my clit with her fingers.

I lost all sense of time and place until Lori's mouth left the nipple she'd been laving with attention, and she trailed her lips down my stomach. When she raised up enough to tug down my boxers, I tried to sit up. "What...what are you doing? No. You don't really have to—"

She looked up at my face. "Shh. Relax."

I did as I was told...for about five seconds. She got the boxers off and went right back to what she'd been about to do. When her tongue circled my clit, rockets went off in my head. I arched into her face.

Without her tongue leaving my clit, Lori shifted from beside me to a position between my legs. I felt like I could feel every nerve ending in my clit. My legs shook. I'd never felt anything so good, so intense. And then it got more intense. Lori kept licking and sucking as she inserted a finger into the opening of my vagina.

I'd brought myself to orgasm before. This was different. I

was about to cum. I heard my own voice call out, "More. Deeper!"

Lori stopped licking and looked up at me. "I don't want to hurt you."

I rolled my head from side to side. "You won't."

"You're sure?"

I could only say, "Riding. Horses." The waves were starting to recede as she waited for my response, but when her mouth and finger returned to their former places, they came roaring back.

When Lori added a second finger and stroked as deep inside me as she could all while flicking my clit with her talented tongue, I went over the edge. It was the longest orgasm I'd ever had, far longer than anything I'd ever been able to give myself with my own hand, even while I pictured those two women in that car. I came then. I'd never done that either.

Lori slowed down as the waves subsided for me, but my legs felt like they were on full vibrate. I couldn't control the shaking. I didn't even want to.

She pulled herself up alongside me and smiled as she curled into the crook of my arm. I couldn't figure out the look she was giving me.

"What?"

"You're amazing."

"Me? I'm still laying here, spread eagle, trying to get control of myself, especially my legs. *You* did that."

She leaned up on one elbow and looped her right leg over mine. "Is that a bad thing?" she asked as she used her free hand to play with one of my nipples again.

"Um, no."

"Well, buckle up, because that was just a start. I have a few more things to show you. Should take a couple of hours, then we'll have a test."

"I have to admit, I've never been a very good test taker."

"Study hard. Think of it like softball. You've got to get from base to base to score."

I scored over and over that night. We both did. It was a tied ball game!

ABOUT THE AUTHOR

Anne Hagan is the author of over twenty works of fiction in the mystery, romance and thriller genres. She writes of family, friends, love, murder, and mayhem in no particular order and often all in the same story. She's a half owner of the weekly discount eBook newsletter, MyQueerSapphFic, a wife, parent, foster parent, and an Army veteran. Anne draws from all of those experiences when she writes because truth is often stranger than fiction.

- Website: https://AnneHaganAuthor.com

- Facebook: https://www. facebook.com/AnneHaganAuthor/

- Twitter: https://twitter.com/AuthorAnneHagan

- MyQueerSapphFic: https://www. myqueersapphfic.com/

IN YOUR HANDS

JOHANA GAVEZ

Could you forget how to have sex? Manuela didn't think so, but she was having her doubts. It'd been so long since she had sex with anybody, she wasn't sure where she would start if an opportunity presented itself. Not that there were any prospective for sexy times in her future besides her own fingers and trusty sex toys like the silver bullet vibrator that never failed her, or the glass dildo she used when she craved more.

Many times in the past few months, she'd considered signing up for a dating app or going out to a club and try to pick someone up, but every time she dismissed the idea. Sex had never been just sex for her. She always needed the emotional connection, the possibility of more, even if it ended not happening, to get herself to open to the possibility of physical touch with another human being, and for the last couple of years she hadn't been ready, but she'd been craving the touch of another more and more lately.

She thought back to the last few times she felt the warm breath of another woman close to her lips. With her eyes closed, she could almost remember how soft lips felt against her skin. How firm hands held her closer, hips touched, thrust, rubbed together in a dance to the rhythm of deep breaths, sighs, and moans. She recalled the memory of a deep, passionate kiss, full of tongue and desire and as the memory filled her mind, she pushed her hips against the bed, grinding her legs together and searching for friction against the firm mattress. The ghost of a past lover hovered over her in the form of a blurry memory without a face, a mix of women now long gone.

One, two, three thrusts against the mattress and the pressure built up in her belly, down her core. The liquid heat of her arousal coated her labia. She could feel it. Smell it. Her hands gripped the sheets and her hips pressed harder against the bed one, two, three times. As she had done so many times before, except those times there was a body moving under her, grasping at her shoulders, begging for more. She pushed down again, each time the pressure sent a bolt of electricity to her core and up her body. She would have liked to have someone biting her neck or licking her nipples, sucking on them hard to awake her senses. Instead, she used her left hand to grab her own breasts and teased her nipples with her index and ring finger, rubbing up and down her already perky nub.

She could come just from grinding. But the urge to have her wetness coat her fingers overwhelmed her. She slid them up and down her entrance at first, feeling the slickness between her fingers, enjoying how wet she'd made herself. Then, one finger teased her clit, softly, slowly, just how she liked it. She would have liked to have an expert tongue do it instead. There was nothing more erotic for her than seeing a woman buried between her legs, drinking up her essence, building her up with firm strokes; except maybe being the one enjoying the taste of arousal, hands pushing her closer, keeping her in place as she drank up the wetness. She didn't have either of those things at the moment, but the memory of them was enough to make her body react.

Her index finger circled her clit without respite, a soft touch that built a strong but calm current of pleasure inside of her. Pleasure rolled from her core to every corner of her body in a measured and controlled way. The release relaxed her muscles and eased her mind. For a long thirty seconds, her mind emptied of any and all thoughts. It was a good start to the night, but she wanted more.

She reached for the smooth glass dildo she'd placed on top of a towel on the bedside table earlier. The cold glass contrasted with the warmth of her skin, waking up her nerve terminals even more than they already were. The extra lube was unnecessary, but it never hurt to use it. She pressed the dildo against her skin, feeling the contrast of the coldness as she moved it up the inside of her leg all the way to her throbbing center. She only used the tip of the dildo at first, teasing her entrance, pushing it inside only a little, almost nothing. Her other hand kept circling her clit at a steady pace, building up the sensations inside her body.

The glass slid without resistance inside her when she pushed it further up. She let out a gasp that turned into a moan as she pressed the curved edge of the glass over her most sensitive area. Soon she developed a rhythm. Her left hand handed the dildo, going in and out, pressing inside her and doing it all over again, while her right hand focused on her clit.

She loved the sensation of being filled up. It'd taken a fair amount of trial and error to find a dildo she loved, not too big, just the right size, until she tried the glass options. She could never go back after that. It was perfect. She loved how it filled her, the easy way it slid in and out of her, and how she could cool it down and have that added sensory load. The room filled with her moans. Low, ragged moans mixed with heavy breathing that got shallower as she increased the pace of her movements.

As the tension inside of her increased, it became harder to maintain the pace and coordinate the movements of both of her hands, but it didn't matter. She was so close, even the occasional slip up of her hand, the slight pause when she lost her focus, wasn't enough to prevent the delicious tension inside of her. She rode the waves for as long as she could. Her fingers rubbing her clit softer, slower, but without stopping until the last wave of pleasure crossed her body.

The world faded around Manuela. Her ears, her eyes, closed off to the world. She stared at the plain white paint on the ceiling but didn't see it. Everything around her was a blur; her senses numbed in a complacent rest. Her eyelids grew heavy, and she knew that letting sleep claim her right after her self-love session would lead to a night of deep and restful slumber, but instead of letting her consciousness fade away, she forced her eyes open and shook away the drowsiness. She reached for the phone, opening the profile she'd filled early in the day on the latest dating app but that she'd never gotten around to publish.

She'd added two selfies that had taken her way too much time to take. It was embarrassing how many pictures she took before settling for the two that, if not great, at least made her look the best she could. One was a smiling picture, lying in bed, half of her face covered with a curtain of hair and her trusty gray cat, Cleo, getting in the way. The second picture was a classic selfie, with her looking seductively, or at least she hoped it looked that way, at the camera and leaning forward to show off her ample cleavage.

It felt awkward and silly, but she wanted to put herself out there, and a dating app was the easiest way. She lost nothing by trying. The hardest part was settling on a bio. After hours of staring at the box without a single idea coming to her mind, followed by writing and deleting at least the first five tries, she settled on something direct since no matter how much she tried, she couldn't come up with something flirty or funny.

32-year-old lesbian that loves eating out and binge-watching TV Shows. Do you want to do those things with me?

She flipped through a dozen profiles, swiping left and right without paying much attention to the details of each profile. With a long, drawn-out sigh, she closed the app and dropped her phone face down on the bed. Publishing the profile was only the start, but she didn't have the energy to chat someone up that night. She dragged her body under the covers and let sleep take over.

"Eating out at a restaurant or the other kind? ;) I'm interested either way."

Manuela stared at the message again. It was there when she woke up almost at noon, teasing her first as a blinking notification on her phone, and then in the app's chat once she opened it up. She was glad there was no way for the other person to know when someone read a message, because she'd been staring at it without answering for way too long. Not because she didn't want to. The message was funny and flirty, everything she would have wanted to put on a first message but would never occur to her. She hadn't even realized the double connotations of using the expression "Eating out" until she read the message.

Sophia. That was the name of the woman that messaged her. Manuela spent more time than she cared to admit looking at her pictures, captivated by the six photographs she'd posted on the app. In each of them, Sophia's big, wide, brown eyes stared back at the camera with a confidence that made it seem like she was looking right at her. She had light brown hair, styled in a ponytail in most of them, but when she let it fall loose, the most adorable curls framed her face. The pictures were outside, hiking, or at parks, and a big, muscled dog, a Pitbull, featured on several of them. Going outside and dogs weren't Manuela's favorite things, but the deep brown eyes were captivating enough to make her want to reply.

The only reason she hadn't answered yet was that, again, she didn't know how to convey in a short text message everything she wanted. She'd never been good at flirting and despite everyone saying it was easier to do it over text, she was finding it to be just as hard.

"I'm also interested in both types of eating out."

She didn't love her reply. Cringed a little at it, to be honest. But at least she'd sent something. As soon as she hit sent, she dropped the phone and focused on something else to disperse the nervous energy cursing through her body. She cooked, cleaned, and exercised until her muscles burned. It wasn't until she came out of the shower, hair wet and clinging to her back, clad in a white, fluffy towel, that she noticed the blinking notification on her phone. She sat on the bed and opened the message with her heart thundering inside her ribcage.

"In general, or with me? ;)"

Manuela bit her lip. She was successfully flirting, and she liked the fluttering it caused inside her stomach.

"I don't know you that well yet. But I'm open to changing that and seeing how it goes."

Even though Sophia's message had arrived only half an hour before, she didn't expect to get another reply soon. When her phone chimed again, only a couple minutes after she replied, a smile spread across her face.

"What do you want to know?"

Fuck. What did she want to know? Her finger hovered over the phone while she mulled over her next words in her mind. She wanted to keep things sexy, but she also wanted to know more about who Sophia was as a person. How compatible they could end up being beyond some casual flirting.

"Top three celebrity MILFs if you're into MILFs," she finally sent.

She stared at the small dots blinking at the edge of the screen, telling her that Sophia was typing. Less than 30 seconds later, she got an answer. "Of course I am. Who isn't? Are you a MILF?"

"No, I'm not," Manuela smiled as she moved her thumbs over the blinking letters on her phone screen. "Disappointed? Also, you didn't answer the question."

"Not disappointed, just curious. As for your question. Only three? Charlize Theron, Angelina Jolie, a little cliché but a classic and I loved her as a baby gay, and Rachel Weisz. Yours?"

Manuela stopped for a second to remember all of her celebrity crushes. She'd had many over the years, but there were some that stood up more than others. "Michelle Yeoh, I would give her anything she wanted if she asked. Salma Hayek and Jennifer Beals."

She was trying to think of what else to say to keep the conversation alive when another message from Sophia popped up.

"Those are some great choices, but now I'm worried."

Manuela frowned. "Worried about what?"

"They're all very attractive women, but now I don't think I'm your type, and that's a shame because you're definitely mine."

She shouldn't have been surprised at how fast the conversation turned flirty. It was a dating app, after all, but it impressed her how smoothly Sophia transitioned from casual messages to something more daring. It was only fair for her to match her energy. She wanted to match her energy.

"I don't have a type and let me assure you, there's no reason for you to worry."

"Oh? Say more. Why not?"

The butterflies in her stomach fluttered stronger than ever. Not necessarily because of Sophia, but having someone's attention, the possibility of something happening was refreshing after so long not daring to try.

"I think you're very attractive." Manuela answered, no seeing any reason to deny the truth.

"Attractive like you would watch me from afar or attractive like you would hit on me if you meet me at a bar and we would end up the night kissing?"

Sophia was fantastic at this whole flirt by text thing and Manuela was glad she was. Made things easier for her, too. "I don't think I'm smooth enough to pick up someone in a bar, but in a hypothetical scenario, I would want to kiss you at the end of the night."

"How would you kiss me?"

Manuela chuckled. She could only admire the ease with which Sophia led the conversation, now venturing it into risky, sexy texts. "How would you want me to kiss you?"

"I don't know. So far, you seem like someone who would start soft and slow. Someone gentle that would tease me at first and drive me nuts with expectation. That could be nice, but I think I would want you to kiss me hard and fast first. Really, show me you're desperate for my touch."

Her reaction was instant. As soon as she read the words, wetness pooled between her legs. Maybe this whole dating app thing wasn't such a bad idea. It may not turn into more than a sexting session, but even if it didn't turn into more than that, she couldn't deny she was enjoying it.

"I can do either of those. I'm very versatile. But I must admit, I enjoy the slow, teasing kisses more." Manuela texted back.

"I wouldn't mind having you teasing me."

Manuela took a deep breath. Despite the messages threading in dangerous territory already, she still got nervous as she wrote the next one. The previous ones were right on the edge of provocative but vague enough there was room to go back. The next one pushed her past that line. "What would you want me to do to you?"

The tree blinking dots moved, and moved, and moved.

Disappeared and appeared again, making Manuela's stomach drop as she waited.

"I want you to hold my hands in place and kiss me. Really kiss me like you mean it. Not a tentative, slow kiss but one full of force and tongue and teeth."

Closing her eyes was all she needed for the visual to take over her brain. The faceless ghost she'd seen in her dreams, in her fantasies before, changed, morphed into someone she could recognize. The brown hair, the red lips she'd seen in Sophia's profile pictures mixed with the features she'd grown so used to seeing in her dreams to form a new woman. One that felt closer, more real, less like a ghost from the past.

"I can do that. I would love to do that. Get on top of you and grind against your leg as my tongue explores your mouth."

Almost without realizing, Manuela pushed her hips down on the mattress. The pressure wasn't enough to satisfy the tension building in her lower belly, the movement only increased her arousal. It was like a fan to a flame.

"What else?" Sophia replied after a couple of minutes.

The reply took longer than before, and Manuela wondered why. If maybe Sophia was also thinking about her somewhere else in the city, pushing her legs together or letting her hand roam around her body.

"I would only kiss you at first. Build you up with a mix of deep kisses and the tip of my tongue exploring the roof of your mouth, teasing the corners of your lips, and then going back to do it all over again. Then I would move to your neck. I would bite hard on it until you cry out in a mix of pain and pleasure."

There was more she could say, but she paused there. She wanted to give Sophia a chance to read and react.

"Fuck, I would love that. I love to get a little rough."

"How rough?"

"Let's say I wouldn't mind you taking control and biting all over my body, if that's what you wanted."

Manuela visualized herself doing just that. Going down Sophia's body, leaving her mark behind. Alternating soft, placid kisses with deeper ones, followed by a mix of soft and harder bites. A soft kiss around Sophia's chest, a deep kiss on her ribcage, a hard bite on the corner where her waist meets her hip.

"Then I'm going to bite all over your body. Down your chest and waist, your inner thighs, and hips. Anywhere I can reach, I'll make you remember it was mine." She didn't give Sophia time to answer. She'd been grinding her hips, looking for fiction as they texted, and as fun as the messages were, she wanted more.

"What are you doing right now?" it was a basic, cliché question, but it worked. She needed to know.

"I'm sure you know what I'm doing."

"I want you to tell me," Manuela insisted.

"I have my hand down my pants and I'm rubbing myself senseless, wishing it were you."

That was all Manuela needed to hear to do the same.

"Good, that's the same thing I'm doing now." And it was true. Her fingers slid over her throbbing clit, rubbing it without pause.

An idea struck her as she got closer and closer to the release she now craved. She'd never done it before, and part of her questioned the sensibleness of following through on an idea she had with her head hazy with pleasure. But there was no time to doubt. With the free hand, she raised the phone as high as her hand allowed and took a picture that showed her bare abdomen, the chest hidden by her long hair and her hand between her panties. At least she was aware enough to make sure her face wasn't visible at all, even so, sending it was still bolder than anything she'd ever done before.

The response was better than she expected. First a text.

"Fuck, you're stunning and you look so hot like that," Sophia responded. Then a picture of her own. Sophia used a full body mirror positioned right in front of the bed for her picture. She was on her knees, wearing nothing. One hand squeezed her chest, and the other covered her center. The hand didn't allow for anything explicit to be shown, but it also made it clear that she had at least two fingers buried deep inside of her, and that realization sent another wave of arousal down Manuela's body.

Sophia went a step further and after the picture, sent her a voice memo recording. When she hit play on it, a string of ragged breaths and deep moans filled the room. Manuela kept the pressure on her clit until her own moans mixed with the ones coming from the recording as she let the waves of pleasure crash over her body. After five minutes of recovering, she wiped her hand on the sheets before firing another text.

"That was great. I hope is not the last time we do it."

Three blinking dots. "I hope next time I can come in your mouth."

Manuela chuckled. Sophia wasn't playing around, and she liked that.

"That can be arranged."

Two strangers in a bar looking at each other from afar. That's what they were. Manuela's eyes moved up and down slowly, taking in the form fitting clothes clinging right to every corner of a blond-haired woman's body. Her gaze followed pink lips as they kissed the edge of a scotch glass, she could see the tip of a tongue in the distance, licking the aftertaste of whiskey and, making Manuela wonder if they'd taste as good as they looked if she kissed them. She took a sip of her own drink, a margarita. It wasn't as elegant or grown up as whiskey, but she liked the taste, and it gave her the buzz she was looking for. She wasn't drunk and didn't want to be, and the one margarita she'd drank so far wasn't enough to fully lower her inhibitions and push her to cross the bar and talk to the woman she'd been staring at for a while now, or maybe it was. She took another long sip, finishing the last drops of liquid on her glass.

Seeing her opening, she moved between the mass of people to reach the spot on the bar where the woman she'd been looking at was sitting. She slid right next to her, trying to not make her intentions too obvious. Not yet. She called the bartender and ordered another margarita, aware the entire time of the pair of eyes fixed on her. She bit down the smile that threatened to take over her lips and turned around slowly.

"Sorry for being all in your space." She offered.

She moved away, even though it was the last thing she wanted, but a hand on her arm stopped her.

"I don't mind," the woman raised her glass in Manuela's direction. "I could use the company."

This time, Manuela didn't stop the smile from spreading over her lips. "I'm happy to keep you company," she raised her own glass. "I'm Manuela, by the way."

"Sophia."

Manuela lost herself for a second in Sophia's intense, unwavering gaze. She knew Sophia was doing it on purpose, daring her almost. They'd talked about it during the days after their first texting session. When they agreed to meet in person, Sophia insisted on not settling for a simple date. She proposed the idea of pretending to be strangers that crossed paths in a bar. A kind of role play. Manuela accepted because it sounded fun. They were pretty much strangers, so it shouldn't be hard to pretend. Now, confronted with the reality of trying to seduce a stranger in a bar, even if she knew Sophia was open and willing to be seduced, she found it harder than she expected. She was rusty. But she wouldn't let that stop her.

"How's the night treating you?" Manuela lowered her voice and tried to use her most seductive tone.

"Better now that you're here."

Manuela chuckled. A low chuckle, a mix of embarrassment and amusement. Sophia was so much smoother than her.

"And I just got here, still haven't shown you just how much better I can make your night."

Sophia leaned closer. "Show me," she breathed out in Manuela's ear.

Manuela took a long sip of her drink and made it a point to slowly lick the aftertaste from her lips as she stared at Sophia. "Let's dance." She stood up and walked away without looking back in a way she'd have never had the courage to do if she didn't already know Sophia would follow her. She only turned around when she got to the dance floor. When she did, Sophia was right behind her. Without wasting time, she placed her hands on Sophia's hips and pulled her closer.

The music barely registered in her brain. She didn't care about it, she only cared about the closeness of their bodies and the way their heat mixed as they swayed together. Sophia was shorter than her, or maybe it was the thick heel of her boots making her stand a few inches above her. It didn't matter; it was perfect since Sophia seemed happy to rest her head on her shoulder, the hot breath coming out of her mouth with every breath making the small hairs of Manuela's neck stand up and a trail of goosebumps travel from her ear, down her neck and arms.

Their hips moved in sync with the music, and with each

other. Sophia didn't talk and Manuela didn't feel the need to talk either. She was happy holding Sophia in her arms, guiding her steps. She rested her hand on Sophia's waist, her thumb tracing a soft patch of exposed skin above her waistband. The curves of their bodies seemed to meld perfectly against each other, and Manuela wondered if they would fit just as perfectly once they moved from the dance floor to a horizontal position. She couldn't wait to find out, but she didn't dare to propose a change of location just yet. Not because she thought Sophia wouldn't accept, but because she was enjoying their literal and figurative dance.

The middle of the dance floor wasn't the most private area, but everyone around them was too busy in their own world to care what they did, and Manuela was feeling bold that night. Her left hand pulled Sophia even closer against her body while her right one traveled down, until it found the edge of her dress and then moved up under the fabric, not much, only enough to feel the heat radiating from Sophia's legs and the softness of her skin. She leaned down and kissed Sophia's neck. She sucked at her pulse point and then left a trail of pecks over her shoulder.

Sophia hummed when Manuela's lips latched onto her neck again.

"You're not playing fair," she said, with a low husky tone that made Manuela smile.

"What am I doing?" Manuela said and then pushed her lips against Sophia's neck and dragged her teeth over the sensitive skin.

Sophia hummed again. "You know exactly what you're doing."

She moved away from Sophia's neck to look into her eyes. She licked her lips while staring at her and then moved her mouth to speak right next to her ear. "Maybe, and there's so much more that I want to do." She said in a low, deep tone. "Do you want to get out of here?"

Sophia didn't answer with words. She grabbed Manuela's hand and led her away from the crowd and out of the bar without looking back.

The first thing she noticed when they made it to Sophia's bedroom was the full body mirror standing right next to the dresser. It didn't reflect the bed as it was positioned right to the side of it, a fact Manuela was glad for since she wasn't ready to have their entire night activities reflected at her, but it was still there, tempting, available if they ever felt like using it. She forgot about it when Sophia's lips latched onto hers, sucking on her lower lip and pulling her from the collar on her plaid shirt as she walked.

She followed with no resistance, her feet occasionally getting tangled in a rug or an uneven floorboard, threatening to make her fall, but she would have fallen on top of Sophia, anyway. Her hands found their home on Sophia's waist, pulling her close so their cores touched as they walked, just like they had while they danced. Her fingers dug into the soft flesh and then moved up towards her back and then her neck. Every movement with only one goal, to bring them closer, to feel more.

The bed was so close, yet so far away. Only a couple of steps they didn't manage to take because they were too engrossed in each other. Manuela grabbed a nearby wall to stabilize them after another stumble and once her fingers felt the solid surface, the rest of her body moved on autopilot to turn Sophia around and press her against the wall. Their bodies couldn't be closer together, but it wasn't enough. She wanted more. Needed more.

Her hands moved to Sophia's legs and from there slid up. Once she reached the hem of Sophia's pants, she traced the soft skin exposed along the edge of the fabric, and Sophia shivered under her touch.

"Take me to bed," she said breathlessly into Manuela's ear and Manuela had to bite down a moan at the obvious want in her voice.

"Why?" she answered, her words also mixed with ragged breaths. "I'm having fun right here." She leaned down and licked the exposed neck so close to her lips.

Sophia moaned and leaned into the touch, craning her neck to give her more access.

"I'm having a lot of fun too, but I want you on top of me," she answered, but her hand moved to Manuela's head, holding her in place as she licked and bit the sensitive skin.

She could have lost herself in Sophia's neck for hours. Encouraged by the string of sighs, hums and moans that came out of Sophia's mouth after each one of her touches, but Sophia's words painted an image in Manuela's head that she couldn't resist. She moved away, only a couple of inches, enough to look into Sophia's eyes and see how dark her pupils had gotten with arousal. "That's a compelling argument," Manuela said and took a step back.

She walked backwards, never breaking eye contact with Sophia, who bit her lower lip as she looked at Manuela from top to bottom, undressing her with her eyes.

When Sophia moved forward Manuela grabbed her, pushed her down on the bed and climbed on top of her just as Sophia had asked her to do. She held herself up on her forearms long enough to look into Sophia's eyes and caught a glimpse of the pure lust dancing in her eyes before the other woman reversed the roles on her before she could react. With one swift movement, Manuela found herself under Sophia.

She smirked but didn't fight the movement. "I thought you wanted me on top," she drawled.

"I changed my mind." Sophia looked into her eyes as she spoke. "You look great from up here, too."

This time Manuela let out a loud chuckle. "Do I? I'll have to see that sometime."

"Kinky, I like it," Sophia winked and leaned down to capture Manuela's mouth in a deep kiss.

Firm, insistent, sensual. She could have used those three words to describe both Sophia and the way she was kissing her. For a second she considered putting up a fight, trying to turn Sophia around and take the control from her, but she couldn't bring herself to do it. She was happy in the position she was. She enjoyed the way Sophia teased her, build up a rhythm and slowed back down within the kiss. Her body was reacting, her wetness obvious between her legs. As Sophia kissed her, Manuela let her hands wander up and down her body. They slid down her sides and legs, only to move back up along her hips and back and then down again.

She fought against her need to feel more of Sophia at first. She didn't want to show her eagerness, her pure and raw need, but it was a lost battle from the start. The second or third time her hands made the journey up from the sides of Sophia's thighs to her ass, she couldn't stop the urge, the need to feel more of Sophia, to have her even closer. She pushed her down, pressing their centers together and creating enough pressure for both of them to let out a simultaneous moan into each other's mouth as they never broke their kiss.

The heat radiated from every one of her pores and the wetness between her legs keep growing, her panties ruined. She wasn't even sure why she was still wearing panties when all she wanted was to feel Sophia's skin against her own, have their wetness's mix as they rubbed against each other. When Sophia let go of her mouth to move her attention to her neck, she took the opportunity to ask for what she wanted.

"I need these clothes gone," she said, her hands tugging at the hem of Sophia's shirt.

Sophia laughed and buried her head in Manuela's neck again. Slowly raking her teeth down the sensitive skin. Manuela almost forgot about her request, too distracted by the prickling extending over her entire body from her head to her chest and down her stomach until it reached her center. Thankfully, Sophia didn't forget it, and soon she moved up, pulling Manuela's shirt up and leaving a trail of kisses as she exposed her skin. Once the shirt was out of the way, she repeated the action, this time moving down, bringing down Manuela's pants and getting rid of any piece of fabric covering her and replacing it with wet kisses that left goosebumps all over Manuela's skin.

Sophia then took her own clothes with little preamble. It was quick and effective. Manuela barely had any time to enjoy the view before the other woman was back on top of her. Again, she considered for one instant the possibility of switching up their positions, but dismissed the idea as soon as it came. She enjoyed the attention. After so much time taking care of herself, she liked the way Sophia led her. There would be time later to change the roles, but at that moment she wanted to enjoy and let someone else decide about her pleasure.

Sophia didn't waste time either. She seemed happy with their roles, too. She hovered over Manuela with a devilish smile on her face. "What should I do first?" She asked.

Sophia's breasts hung right over Manuela's chest, the tips of their nipples touching and making it hard for Manuela to focus. On instinct, her hands went to Sophia's ass. This time, she didn't bother with being subtle. She grabbed Sophia's ass cheeks, her fingers digging into the soft skin, and pushed down. That was all it took for Sophia to get the message. She started grinding against Manuela's center, matching the pace Manuela set.

Her grunts and moans mixed. The pressure in her stomach grew.

"Fuck," she moaned out.

"The way you move is so fucking sexy," Sophia breathed out. "You look so hot right now." She added and let out a moan when Manuela used her hands to bring their cores even closer.

They fell into a rhythm. Sophia moved on top of her, back and forth, up, and down, pressing her down against the bed, rubbing their centers against each other. Manuela matched her every thrust with one of her own, her hands never leaving her waist so she could lead her to press harder or faster, depending on what she needed, staring into each other's eyes as they moved. She tried to close her eyes, overwhelmed by the closeness and the intensity of Sophia's gaze, but she ended up opening her eyelids back up after less than a second, unable to look away.

The loud sound of their panting accompanied each thrust of their hips. The pressure in her lower abdomen increased, tingles shooting from her core to the edge of her hair and fingertips every time Sophia's center rubbed against hers. She closed her eyes and let the sensations engulf her body. She allowed herself to feel every tingle, every speckle of pleasure traveling up and down her anatomy. Her first instinct was to fight the feeling, to try to prolong the experience as much as she could before succumbing to the inevitable pleasure. Why? An irrational fear of the night ending way too soon. It was a losing battle from the start, and to be fair, she didn't fight that hard. The waves of pleasure, the weight of Sophia on top of hers, the cadence of her hips against her own, the warmth of her breath and the desire in her eyes all colluded to push her over the edge.

She arched her back and clung to Sophia's shoulders, digging her nails hard enough that the other woman let a subtle cry mixed with a moan as electricity shot through Manuela's entire body.

Through her numbed senses, through the haze of pleasure, she felt Sophia's lips on her skin. Felt the plump lips leaving a wet trail of saliva over her shoulders and neck. Sophia whispered something in her ear, but her brain was too far gone still to understand. As her awareness returned, the desire to taste Sophia, to have her come undone under her in the same way she just had, increased.

"Lay down," she instructed, shifting her weight to push Sophia away from her body and onto the mattress.

Sophia raised an eyebrow and smiled, letting Manuela put her exactly in the position she wanted.

"What do you have in mind?" the other girl said, her voice low and raspy.

Manuela said nothing at first. She used one of her fingers to follow the trail of Sophia's skin from her chest, down to her stomach, and lower. "I want to taste you, unless you rather I do something else."

They'd gotten STD tested before meeting in person to make sure they were safe, that gave them more liberty to explore whatever type of touch they felt like exploring and what Manuela wanted was to coat her tongue with Sophia's wetness and savor the delicious taste, fill her nostrils with the smell of sex, of want, of need. Sophia nodded and opened her legs wider as an invitation. Manuela didn't waste time making her way down. She used her tongue to travel the length of Sophia's body. First, she spent as much time kissing, licking, sucking on her nipples and sides, her stomach and hips, her thighs, and her legs as she planned to spend enjoying her sex.

Sophia squirmed under her, her legs opening wider as Manuela got closer to her center, as her kisses moved from the inside of her thighs to her swollen lips and took the little numb begging for her attention between her lips. The moans and the hand grasping at her hair encouraged her to keep a steady pressure over the numb, but she couldn't help but let go of it for a second to lick all the wetness pooling between Sophia's legs and then tease her entrance with the tip of her tongue.

Sophia groaned at first, when Manuela's lips let go of her clit, but she went back to whimpering in pleasure when she pushed the tip of her tongue inside her. The taste on her taste buds was everything Manuela craved and once she got what she wanted, she turned her attention back to the little nub, asking for it.

Quietness turned out to not be one of Sophia's qualities. She was so vocal, and Manuela loved every minute. The moans, the demands, the breathy petitions for more, filling her with purpose. Sophia also wasn't good at staying in place. She moved and trashed in reaction to every stroke of Manuela's tongue, to the point it forced her to grab Sophia's hips and use her strength to keep her in place.

It was funny to see the contrast between her desperation one second and then the way an instant later how she let out a muffled moan that seemed to get caught in her throat and her body went lip. Manuela slowed down but didn't stop until she felt Sophia was truly and utterly spent and finished. At that point, she moved up her body, licking her lips to catch the last vestiges of wetness from her lips and finished by kissing an adorably tired Sophia who, despite her hooded eyes and limp muscles didn't hesitate to suck on Manuela's tongue.

"Ummm," Sophia let out. "That wasn't half bad."

Manuela laughed, rolling away from Sophia. "Not half bad? I'll take that," she said, pulling the sheet over her body.

It didn't occur to her until after she'd settled on the bed and her eyes were getting heavy with sleep that Sophia may have wanted her to leave, but she didn't have the energy and since she wasn't kicked out, she was going to assume she was welcome to stay. At least for a couple of hours.

While she got dressed, Manuela sneaked glances at Sophia, who was still splayed on the bed, fully naked. She was aware she was overstaying her welcome, but her desire to spend more time with Sophia won over her fear of being rejected.

"We never got around to the other kind of eating out," she said to break the ice. Her voice was steady despite the way her heart raced inside her chest.

Sophia looked at her a small smile on her lips, her head tilted and her eyes narrowing slightly. The thirty or so seconds it took her to give her answer felt like an eternity. Manuela was already bracing herself for an outright rejection or a noncommittal answer they both would know it was only to avoid an awkward moment when Sophia finally spoke.

"There's a new Thai place I've been dying to try out. How's next Friday?"

She swallowed the knot that had formed in her throat. "Next Friday sounds perfect." She took a deep breath. "But what about brunch today?"

She knew she may be asking for too much, but she wanted to give it a try. She still expected to be rejected but asking to spend time together right away made clear her intentions and Sophia could decide to meet her halfway or let her down gently.

"I guess I better get my cute ass out of bed and ready so we can make it to Hugo's the absolute best brunch spot in the city before there's a line the size of Texas."

When Sophia jumped out of bed, not caring to cover herself, and ran naked to the bathroom, Manuela had to fight the urge to stop her to plant a kiss on her lips. She looked adorable running like that. It was only brunch, it didn't have to mean anything, but Manuela couldn't help the silver of hope that took hold in her heart.

"I'll be ready in twenty," Sophia screamed from the bathroom. Suddenly, her head peeked out from the side of the door. "Does this count as our first date or is it technically the second?"

Manuela's mouth hung open at first, at a loss for words. Of course, Sophia would ask directly if she meant for brunch to be a date. "I think it counts as a first date, but we can decide the technicalities later."

Sophia winked. "Sounds like a plan."

ABOUT THE AUTHOR

Johana is a proud Colombian that loves losing herself in stories and fantasy worlds. She loves watching cooking shows, even though she can barely cook, and spending relaxing afternoons reading in her hammock. At risk of becoming a stereotype, she loves to listen to Shakira, Maluma, and J Balvin, but will always choose tea over coffee. Her writing is centered on Sapphic stories with romance at their core. She loves fluffy novels where love always wins.

- Website: https://www.johanagavez.com/

- Facebook:
  https://www.facebook.com/johanagavezauthor

- Twitter: https://twitter.com/johanagavez

- Instagram:
  https://www.instagram.com/johanagavez/

MY EDINBURGH AWAKENING

KITTY MCINTOSH

Finding myself wandering the ancient cobbled streets of Edinburgh alone was not in my plan. Six weeks ago, I had taken the train from the west coast, hoping to sign a book deal with one of the big publishers, and silence Jade's constant criticisms. Jade, whose support I had taken for granted. Well, you do when that person has stood beside you and sworn to be your everything until death do you part. How wrong was I?

After allowing myself to be gaslit for two years by someone who would appear and disappear as it suited her, I'd had enough of the secrets and lies. I was the last to come to the realization that it wasn't working. Every one of my friends had tried to tell me, but I was stubborn. And in love. However hard I tried, I always felt Jade was hiding something from me and even now, after everything, I still hadn't discovered what it was.

Edinburgh was a strange mixture of the gothic, the Victorian, and the most startling ultra-modern architecture one could imagine. I preferred the old town, where it didn't take much of a stretch to imagine witches of the past shopping for supplies. The dark streets, with lanes snaking off into worlds unknown, had always fascinated me. Now it was home.

My books invariably featured witches. Not surprising considering I was one myself. I had kept that particular fact from Jade, and maybe she had sensed that I was holding something back and resented it. But that was then, and I had a new life to build.

My small flat was on the second floor of a sandstone tenement building near Waverley Station. From my bedroom window I could see the trains coming and going, the crowds thronging the platforms. With so many people around, how could one be lonely? Very easily, I soon discovered. If I was going to make a go of Edinburgh, I had to get myself out there, and that meant meeting new people.

Finding my cupboards quite bare one Sunday morning, I decided it was time to sample the local cafes and tearooms. Maybe I'd meet some like-minded individuals while I was at it. There had to be a coven somewhere in the city. They couldn't all have been wiped out during the Scottish witch hunts. Although it was the early 1700s before they stopped executing witches in Scotland, the suspicion and finger-pointing still went on for many years. Now, of course, society associated witches with nature and healing, so hiding shouldn't be such a problem. Or so I hoped.

If I was being honest, it wasn't just the desire to meet fellow witches that forced me out of my flat and into the real world of Edinburgh. I had an itch to scratch, and as the days went on, I was reminded of just how long it had been since I had had sex.

How should I make myself known to the community I wished to connect with? Certainly my requirements were niche. Lesbian witches need only apply. I'd had enough of hiding and intended to be myself for the first time in my life. Maybe thirty years ago I would have placed a carefully worded ad in a local newspaper. Vague enough not to arouse suspicions in the general populace, but obvious to those who knew what to look for. These days? Was social media the way to go? Or could I still use an old-fashioned method to find my people?

My wanderings around the old town had resulted in many morning coffees since that first outing. In various establishments, with differing levels of success. I needed to find a place I would feel comfortable in, and I was not ready to give up. On the sixth morning I discovered a tiny French cafe, hidden from the throngs of tourists along a dark and windy lane. It came as no surprise that 'La Baguette Magique' or 'The Wand' in English, turned out to be the place I had been looking for. The odd non-magic person would stumble across it, of course, but it would seem like any other French cafe, with a charming owner, and the most delicious patisserie imaginable. Nothing more.

My experience was altogether different. The moment I stepped inside, my life changed. I could see every piece of memorabilia on the walls was a reference to an area of magic. From the corner of my eye, if I looked a certain way, I could see the lights that led to the exact thing I had been seeking. This was a portal, a door into the world I needed to enter.

I did not make myself known to the beautiful woman behind the counter on that first visit. But who was I kidding? For anyone with magical leanings, my true nature would have been obvious. Claudette introduced herself as she took my order. When I asked if she had any gluten-free offerings, she beamed. As a fellow intolerant, she always had an entire shelf of gluten-free cakes and patisserie. Having made a list of the things I would most value in a partner, Claudette had already ticked off three - beautiful, witchy and a great baker. It would take a bit more time to find out if she ticked the one on sexual compatibility.

After a few visits, I felt it was time to make my intentions known. Claudette had continued to be friendly and welcoming, and if I was correct, there was an inkling of more. I had spotted her looking in my direction for a few seconds more than necessary several times. I was not one to push myself forward normally, but my need for a connection was growing more urgent by the day.

As I stood at the glass-fronted counter to pay my bill, I

considered how to start the conversation. Should I come right out with it? Ask her for a date? Or should I be a bit more subtle? Subtle wasn't me, though. Should I mention the obvious witchy element to the cafe? Would that let her know we had rather a lot in common? Before my rational mind had time to stop me, I blurted out, "Would you like to come with me to The Annual Witchcraft Ball?"

A slow, sensuous smile appeared on her face, her deep green eyes sparkling. "I wondered when you were going to pluck up the courage to ask. You've been giving out the most powerful vibes for the past few weeks."

I could feel a crimson tide rise from my neck to my forehead. So, my attempt to appear cool and aloof hadn't worked. She had me worked out from the start.

"One doesn't wish to assume in these matters. I was waiting until I was sure."

"Well, I'm glad you acted now. The Ball is on Saturday night, and I wasn't relishing going on my own. Meet me here at seven on the dot."

———

As the hour of the Ball approached, my nerves kicked in. I had never been 'out' as a witch in my past life and I now knew that had prevented me from fully sharing myself with anyone. As a stranger in Edinburgh, I felt free to be myself. Maybe I could act on some of the fantasies I had, too. Time would tell.

When it came time to pick Claudette up from her flat above the 'La Baguette Magique', nothing could have prepared me for the stunning woman who appeared on the doorstep. Dressed in an emerald green, silk ballgown, with kitten heels to match, she took my breath away. Her copper hair, tied in a chignon, was held in place with a diamond-encrusted comb. The look was timeless, and she would have been just as at home in the 19th century. It occurred to me that maybe she had been around then. Witches were notoriously long-lived, after all. I was 78 years old, but I knew that any non-magic person would put me at around 35.

The Ball was to be held in the Haberdasher's Hall in the heart of the old town. I assumed we would walk there, as it was only a few streets away. Claudette had other ideas. As she took my hand, I felt a shiver go through my entire body, wakening something that had been missing for far too long. She led me to that shimmering light in the corner, the one I could only see if I looked out of the corner of my eye and concentrated. As we approached, I heard her mutter an incantation. A portal opened, leading right into the ballroom.

I had expected to arrive by the front door, keeping everything low key and non-magic. But our arrival at the venue was anything but low key. Heads turned as we walked from the light, and I wondered why we should cause such a stir. It couldn't be anything to do with me. No-one in Edinburgh knew me. So, it must be Claudette. Was she someone famous in the witching community?

As we entered the ballroom, giddiness overcame me at the sight of so many witches in one room. I could never have imagined there were so many of us. Sparkling chandeliers hung from the ceiling, throwing beams of light around the room. Music played just loud enough that I was aware of it, but the overwhelming sound came from the excited chatter of women suddenly free to be themselves. It seemed that I wasn't the only one holding my breath every day in the real world. The room fizzed with the energy of hundreds of women able to live their truth. But something niggled at me.

Turning towards Claudette, I could see something wasn't

right. Gone was the confident, happy woman of a few moments ago in the cafe. Her eyes flitted around the room, as her body took on a stiff, rigid posture. What on earth could be the matter?

Trying to make light of the changed situation, I gently probed, "Why are they staring at us? I know it's my first time here, but surely I can't be the first unfamiliar face to turn up at one of these balls?"

Adjusting her clothes repeatedly, she finally spoke. "It's me they're looking at."

"Why? Are you some sort of superstar witch? A TikTok witch sensation?"

A snort escaped her, as if suddenly snapped out of her agitation.

"Not exactly. Come with me for a minute. I'll try to explain."

Every pair of eyes in the room followed us, and I soon realised there was nowhere to hide from them. As Claudette led me to an unoccupied table in the corner, the women parted, making a path for us. I couldn't work it out.

The table, covered in a pristine white tablecloth, and set for a five course meal, was seriously impressive. A myriad of knives, forks and spoons were laid out in a bewildering manner. I thought my table manners were acceptable, but this was 'dinner-with-the-Queen' fancy. Not my usual type of event.

I tried to block out the stares of every other woman in the room, concentrating my attention on Claudette. She looked decidedly uncomfortable.

"I should have explained, but I wasn't sure how this was going to pan out." She gestured between us, sighing.

"I'm sure it's nothing I can't handle. C'mon Claudette, just tell me."

"O.K., so you know I'm a witch. Obviously. But you've

lived your life outside of the coven structure. How you've managed, I don't know. I've always been part of the community..." Her voice tapered off.

I still couldn't work out where she was going with it. But her discomfort was obvious. So I tried to keep my impatience tamped down.

After a deep inhalation of breath, she started again. "The thing is, I was married."

"Hey, so was I. But the past is the past."

"No, you don't understand. My ex-wife is very important and influential in the community. In fact, she's the High Priestess of the Confederation of Scottish Covens. I was her consort for a very long time. This is the first time I've brought another woman to a public event."

Her behaviour began to make some sense. So, Claudette had been the Prince Philip of the witchy world for years. I could see why it would be weird seeing her with a new partner. It would be like the Duke of Edinburgh stepping out with Kim Kardashian after following two steps behind the Queen for sixty years.

"Right, I get it. But they can't expect you to stay single forever, surely? How long have you been divorced?"

"Five years. She cheated. I don't know who with. All I know is, her claims to be away on Coven business every other week was nonsense. Eventually, I'd had enough and ended it. This lot has never forgiven me."

I leaned across the table and took her hand in mine. "That was then. Over and done with. We're going to get up from this table, heads held high and do whatever it is one does at a witch's ball. This lot will have to suck it up."

I watched her body visibly relax, as if the weight of the world had been lifted. A problem shared and all that. Now the night could really begin. I was keen to find out what the witching community got up to after dark.

After a sumptuous dinner, Claudette rose and beckoned me to follow her to the far end of the room. Several doors led out of the ballroom, but as this was my first time, I did not know where. I noticed other couples doing the same. Had they had put some entertainment on in another room? I was certainly curious at the excitement on the faces of the other women rushing towards the doors. As one door opened to the right, I spotted writhing bodies engaged in what could only be described as the most athletic spectacle of love-making I had ever seen - or imagined. I lost count of the arms and legs involved and realised the ball was a front for an orgy of spectacular proportions.

My pussy throbbed, imagining exactly what was going on in each of the rooms behind the doors. I sneaked a glance at Claudette to see that she was as enthralled and the colour rising on her cheeks told its own story. In that moment, I longed to touch her, to caress her. Her gaze turned towards me and I could have melted on the spot. If eyes are really mirrors to the soul, I could see every want and need in her beautiful green eyes.

This was my chance. Slowly, I ran my fingers down her arm, causing the hairs to rise. Closing the short distance between us, I faced her. Her lips parted, sending a shiver down my spine and setting every nerve ending on fire. I had to get us into one of those rooms. Now!

I gestured towards the last room on the right and searched Claudette's face for a clue. She smiled, slowly and sensuously, nodding her agreement. As she all but dragged me into the room, I was pleased that we agreed on what would come next. I could feel myself becoming wet, the insistent throbbing becoming unbearable. How much longer could I wait to touch her and have her touch me?

We were not alone in the room. Having seen what was going on next door, I was not surprised. Did it bother me? I had never had sex in front of other people before, but the ache between my legs was taking over any rational thought I may have had. There could have been a hundred other women in that room and I wouldn't have cared. I wanted to possess Claudette and know every part of her. I wanted her to scream my name as I made her come over and over again.

On the couches scattered throughout the room, women writhing on almost all of them. I led Claudette to an empty one in the far corner, kissing her as we went. By the time we sat on its edge, I knew I was soaking through my dress. I had never been so turned on in my life. Getting us both naked was a priority. I could only imagine how amazing she would look. She pulled my hands towards her left side, placing my hands on the zipper. I clumsily undid it, so desperate was my need.

It's amazing how easy it is to forget the rest of the world when in the throes of passions. I could only think of Claudette and the impending explosion threatening to send me into oblivion. As I touched and tasted her inch by inch, I was on fire. As much as I wanted it to last as long as possible, my body had other ideas. I could feel Claudette was close, her breathing becoming more rapid. As I looked into her eyes, a mixture of lust and ecstasy stared back at me. As she cried out, I couldn't hold it any longer. Wave after wave of pleasure coursed through me as I held onto her. Our bodies in synch.

As I came down from the most powerful orgasm I had ever experienced, I struggled to focus. It had jolted my brain and my body into another existence. So much so that I thought I could see something that just couldn't be. For there, on the opposite side of the room on another couch, was Jade, engaged in what I could only describe as the most impressive gymnastic feat I'd ever seen. But that was impossible. And not only because she was never remotely athletic or imaginative in bed with me. The main reason I found it hard to believe, though, was the fact that we were attending a ball for witches. And only witches.

Jade could not be a witch. Surely I would know such a thing, wouldn't I? But hang on for a minute. She didn't know I was one, so it was possible. My lightbulb moment! No wonder it didn't work out between us, if we were keeping a secret like that from each other. I always had an inkling that she was holding something back. I just didn't imagine that this was it.

As I came to terms with the implications, I could see Claudette looking at me, then looking at Jade.

"You know Jade?" she spluttered.

"My ex-wife."

Her face turned that oft described 'whiter shade of pale.'

"Mine too."

ABOUT THE AUTHOR

Kitty McIntosh is a writer living on the west coast of Scotland. She writes romance, mystery and erotica as Kitty McIntosh and was most recently published in 'Silk & Leather' from Bold Strokes Books. Her novella, 'Kilbirnie, Scotland' was published in 2019 by Jug Run Press and her short story 'The Woman By The River' went to No.1 in the Amazon Short Reads Chart. 'The Women and The Storm' continued her Tarbet Witches Series. Kitty's stories are inspired by the beautiful countryside and coastal areas around her.

- Website: http://kittykatwordpresscom.wordpress.com

- Facebook: https://www.facebook.com/kitty.author.3

- Twitter: https://Twitter.com/KittyKatAuthor

- Twitter: https://twitter.com/PumpkinAuthor

RETURN OF THE BRAT

KIM HARTFIELD

After half an hour addressing envelopes, the stack of wedding invitations only seemed to have grown. I put down the pen and shook out my wrist. "Why did I decide to do this by hand?" I groaned.

Emery poked her head in the doorway, the hint of a smirk on her heart-shaped lips. "That's exactly what I said last night."

It took me a moment to figure out what she was implying. Last night in bed, she got carried away with her own hands until she was completely drained. When it was my turn, I brought out a few items from the toy collection, and I had one mind-blowing orgasm after another. She sulked for the rest of the night, jealous that I'd enjoyed myself more than her.

"Not my fault," I told her, massaging my wrist.

She stepped into the kitchen, her white and yellow sundress clinging loosely to each curve, her auburn braid dangling in front of one creamy shoulder. "Let me do that for you." Her delicate fingers dug into my forearm, and a shiver ran down my spine. After all our years together, there were no surprises left between us, and yet her touch never failed to affect me.

"For a second, I thought you meant you were going to do the invitations for me."

"I will, just not yet. The wedding is still six weeks away. There's plenty of time." She switched to using her knuckles, pressing rhythmically into my skin.

"Are you kidding?" I dropped my head into my free hand. "Letters take time to deliver! And then people need to RSVP! What if some invitations get lost in the mail?"

"Sara, baby, I've never seen you this stressed." She placed her hands on my shoulders, squeezing them enough to release a tiny bit of tension. "You need to take a break and stop thinking about wedding stuff for a while."

"Not right now." Even if I forgot about the invitations for a while, there were a million and one other things to worry about. I doubted I'd be able to take a break until we were on our honeymoon.

"You know what would help?" She wrapped both arms around me from behind, leaning against me so her breasts grazed my upper back. "Ice cream."

"Seriously?"

"Yes, baby." She draped herself onto my lap, all softness and sweet scent. "I've been craving it all day. The chocolate coconut one from the place I like."

Using all my willpower, I reached past her to grab the pen. "I really want to get these invitations done."

She shook her head, snuggling up to my chest in a way that blocked my hand from moving. "No invitations. Just ice cream."

Reluctantly, I circled my arms around her. Before meeting her, I'd never understood the concept of an Achilles heel. Now I got it. My soft spot for Emery was the size of a small truck, and when she turned on the charm, it was almost impossible to say no to her.

"You can go get it yourself," I said. "Or get it delivered." My resolve was breaking, and I was a hundred percent sure she could hear it.

"Need you there." She rubbed against me. "Ice cream plus Sara equals happy Emery."

I bit my lip, almost ready to give in. God, it was tempting. On the other hand, holding her so close to me was tempting me in a whole other way. Did she have any idea what she did to me?

"Ice cream," she repeated. "Ice cream. Ice cream. Ice cream."

Her cheeky tone flipped a switch inside me, and my decision was made without any further deliberations. I squeezed her hips, my voice roughening. "Do you know what you are? You get three guesses, and if you get it wrong, you're getting punished."

She put on an innocent smile. "An incredible actress. A talented screenwriter. An amazing fiancée."

All of those were true, but not what I was going for. "Nice try." I shifted her into my arms and stood up in one fluid motion. The feel of her body pressed to mine had my heart beating fast, and my core tightened with anticipation as I carried her up the stairs.

She giggled, tilting her head back so her braid flew out behind her. "What am I, then?"

"A brat." I reached the second floor. "A sexy... little... brat."

I deposited her on the bed and her sundress hiked up, showing off miles of smooth skin–and the slightest peek of white panties. She rolled onto her stomach, kicking her feet into the air in a way that made the dress skim up to her ass cheeks. She was still giggling.

"Did I say something funny?" I growled. I wanted to tear that dress right off her body.

She ran a finger along her neckline, slipping a strap off her shoulder. Her dress dipped in front, revealing cleavage that made my head spin. "I had no idea I was a brat. No one has ever said such a thing to me."

"I'm pretty sure I've told you once or twice." More like every day. "If you forgot, I'm going to have to keep telling you."

I climbed onto the bed and turned her over with a push that made her breasts spill out of her dress. My boxer briefs were soaked, and they got even wetter as one hand found the base of her neck. As I pressed down lightly, she sucked in a gasp, her cheeks taking on the pink tinge that was the telltale sign of her arousal.

We both knew our safe words, and we also knew when we

could go full speed ahead. Right now fell into the latter category, and I tightened my fingers around her neck.

"Fine, I'm a brat." Even getting choked, she managed to look calm and collected as she shrugged. "What are you going to do about it?"

I took both her breasts into my hands, squeezing them to the point where she flinched. "I already told you, you're getting punished."

"Duh, I'm asking what's the punishment?" Her pink tongue flickered out to lick her lips, betraying the effect I was having on her.

"Okay, you just made it that much worse." I swatted one breast, and her pretty features flashed with the exact pain-pleasure mix I was looking for. "If you keep talking back, I'm going to add more to your punishment."

"Not very scary when I still don't know what it is."

"For your brattiness downstairs, I'm going to paddle your ass." I swept my fingertips along the smooth skin of her stomach. "And for your smart mouth just now, you're going to thank me while I do it."

Her pupils dilated and she arched her back. "And if I don't?"

I crossed the room and dug through our toy chest, letting the silence stretch out until I came back with our favorite paddle. "You don't want to find out."

"Hmm." She tipped her head to one side, and I could practically see the thoughts running through her mind. Was it worth pushing me harder? She'd already had her fun. What if the next level of punishment was less pleasant? "Fine," she finally said.

"Good girl." I stroked her hair, watching for the hint of glee on her face. As much as she tried to hide it, I could see it every time I praised her. "Now turn over."

"Sure thing, mistress." The smirk she gave me made my eyebrows raise.

Just as I'd suspected, she wasn't done playing games. She turned onto her front... and kept going right onto her back again.

"What's the matter?" she asked, leaning on her elbows so her breasts were thrust directly at me. "You got a problem?"

"You think you're clever? Don't you realize if you stay like this, I'm just going to paddle these?" I ran my fingers along the curve of her breast, finishing with a firm pinch of her nipple.

She grumbled out an acknowledgement and then slowly, resentfully turned over. Her dress was still bunched around her waist, and I grabbed the airy fabric to finally be rid of it. Now the only thing standing between my paddle and her bare flesh was the thin material of her white bikini-cut panties. I caressed her bottom first. I could never look at it without wanting to touch and squeeze and bite it.

"Wow, this is such an awful punishment." Her words dripped with sarcasm. "I'm hating this so much right now."

"Be quiet, brat, or I'll have to shut you up myself." I had no shortage of gags for the times when she was really bad—but that wasn't as fun for either of us. I'd give her one more chance and see if she kept pushing my buttons. Well, maybe two more chances.

"Hmph." She wiggled her butt, glancing back over her shoulder with a pout. "I'm waiting."

I adjusted my position, placing one hand on the small of her back to keep my balance—and to keep hold of her if she tried to fight. She surprised me like that once in a while, and it was always smart to have physical control over her.

For the moment, she was only squirming—and that seemed more like arousal than defiance. I lifted the long, sleek paddle, the leather cool on my skin. The words *Respect Your Mistress* were diamond-encrusted on the back.

I touched the tip to the curve of her butt, more of a tap than a punishment. I was still teasing her, getting her warmed up. The good part was coming, but she had to be patient.

"Are you kidding me?" she demanded with a huff. "Even with a sore hand, you can't do any better than that?"

"I think you forgot to say something."

She heaved a loud sigh. "Thanks a lot."

"Good girl." I gave her a proper smack, though it was still preposterously light. "Now try it without the attitude."

"Thank you," she mumbled.

I paddled her so firmly that a tiny gasp came through her lips. "Say it properly."

Her face was flushed when she looked back at me. "Yeah, yeah, thanks."

"And there's the attitude again." I whacked her hard enough to make her ass cheeks reverberate. My own breath caught in my chest. The sight of her soft flesh bouncing always left me hypnotized.

"Thank you," she said.

She was starting to behave herself, which could only mean one thing. She thought by being good, she could get away with touching herself.

Three... two... one. Right on cue, she shifted to the side so she could slide her hand inside her panties. Then she rolled back on top as if she thought I wouldn't have noticed.

"Did I tell you to masturbate?" I grabbed her arm. "You know fully well you're not allowed yet."

She pressed her face down, her hips sheltering her hand. The little muscles inside her forearm worked furiously as if she was getting in the maximum pleasure that she could before I made her stop. "But you already punished me."

"Oh, you think that was punishment? Baby, I'm just getting started." I pushed her lightly to the side so I could pull her hand away. "You've been acting up more than usual tonight, and for that, you're not going to get to come until I tell you to."

"*What?*" Her face filled with shock–along with a thrill. Edging was always incredibly frustrating for her–and she climaxed harder than ever when I made her do it.

"Sorry, not sorry." I caressed her smooth ass cheek, then pulled the panties down and squeezed hard enough to leave a handprint. "It was your choice to be a brat. You can't tell me you don't deserve it."

"It's not fair." She bit her lip and pouted. "I didn't come enough last night."

"And that was because of your greediness, too." I resumed paddling. "One of these days, you're going to learn to be good."

"Never."

No, she never would–and I wouldn't like it much if she did. Still, I laced my fingers through her hair, giving it a yank just hard enough to sting. "If you want to touch yourself, you know you have to ask me first."

"What if I ask you to do it instead?"

"Then I just might say yes." Gesturing at her to roll over, I eased down to her side. Sliding my fingers over her panties, I sucked in a low hiss. She had completely soaked through the fabric–and as I moved my hand, I could swear I felt more juices gush.

"Touch me for real." The slight catch in her voice betrayed her desperation. "Please."

I circled my fingers slowly, enjoying every second of her torture. "Remember, you're not going to come until I tell you. Don't you want me to hold off?"

She shook her head, her cheeks pink. "I just need to feel you. I swear I won't come."

Despite how much she sassed me, I knew she meant that part. We'd gone over our rules and boundaries years ago, and coming without permission was a line she'd never cross.

I kept up my feathery touch a moment longer, then gave in to her whimpered pleas. Unbelievably, her folds were even wetter than I'd expected, and I dipped my fingers in to lubricate them before moving back up to caress her clit.

"No, no." She grabbed my wrist. "I want you in."

I wouldn't protest that. I would've stayed inside her twenty-four hours a day if I could. I straddled her, extending my first two fingers as her hips rose to meet me. The hot embrace of her center made me shudder, making me crave her touch as well—but right now, my pleasure was secondary to hers.

Slowly, carefully, I slid in to the base of my knuckles. With a moan, she pushed her legs apart, thrusting upward sense-lessly. "More. Give me more."

I eased another finger in, and her walls clenched around me in the most erotic welcome I'd ever experienced. I grazed my thumb over her tight bundle of nerves. "Good?"

Her whole body rocked and her face flushed more as she let out frantic words. "No, no, no. Too much."

I held back a laugh as I tucked back my thumb. My little brat knew touching her there would push her straight over the edge, and for once in her life, she didn't want that to happen. I cupped her breast, squeezing it the way she liked as I thrust slowly, deeply into her. When her breath was ragged and her features were tight, I dipped my head to take one hard, pointed nipple between my lips.

"Oh!"

She thrashed under me—I'd taken her by surprise. Her breasts were so sensitive that playing with them was often all it took to make her orgasm. But I hadn't been thinking about edging. I'd simply wanted to suck on them.

"I'm almost there," she panted. "Can I come?"

"Of course not." A sly grin came over my face.

I knew that she knew I'd never let her come the first time she asked. She was starting early so that I'd give in when she actually wanted to, so the edging wouldn't be too much torture. Unfortunately for her, I could read her body language like a book. I knew how much more she needed, often down to the very second–and she wasn't that close yet.

When two people had been together as long as we had, and when they'd journeyed to the heights of ecstasy over and over, sex became as much mental as physical. I knew the tricks Emery liked to use, and in turn, she knew what I would do to keep her in line. The whole thing had become an erotic game, the tension building incessantly until both of us won.

I caught her nipple between my teeth, teasing it with my tongue as I continued pushing my fingers into her. Her whole body was tight, and she writhed in a way that was immensely satisfying. The tormented moans coming out of her were even better.

"How about now?" she said in a low whine, her eyes filling with desperation.

It was a good try, but not quite good enough. Why weren't her legs shaking? Her toes curling? She could still hold off, and she damn well would. And I'd make it as hard as I possibly could for her.

I lifted my head, angling my hand deeper. "Not yet," I breathed, my own words tight with the force that I was fucking her. "Not... quite... yet."

Her whole face had gone pink, and a bead of sweat appeared on her forehead. Her fists tangled in the bed sheets, her hips rocked along with each solid thrust, and her taut abs were quivering as I continued to fuck her.

"Seriously," she whimpered. "I'm right there. I'm not lying."

I kept burying myself in her relentlessly. She was being honest now. The signs I was looking for were starting to appear–but I had a feeling that my sweet brat could push herself a little further.

I caressed the side of her face, almost sympathetic to the torture she was going through. "Didn't I tell you this was your punishment?"

"I can't keep holding back." Her core contracted around my fingers, only a tremor compared to the spasms of her orgasm. Her body was teetering on the edge of climax without even getting her conscious permission. "Please, Sara, baby, please. I–I–I *need* this."

I'd never pushed things this far, never seen her beg without a shred of brattiness, without even a scrap of dignity. She was all primal energy and animal instinct, any modesty long since forgotten. Whenever she came, it would be nothing less than earth-shattering. The only question was when I would allow that to happen.

"*Please!*" Her hips rose off the bed, both of her hands wrapping around my wrist to force my fingers deeper. "Please, I'll be good! I'll do anything you want me to!"

I liked the sound of that–and I knew she had to be truly desperate to say it. "All right, baby." I tilted my fingertips to her g-spot. "Come for wifey."

Before my words were even out, her body clamped down on me and her juices gushed around my fingers. I lost myself in her pleasure, and her shrieks echoed off the ceiling.

Finally, she sucked in a deep breath and gave my arm a feeble push. I drew out of her and lay down at her side, eager for my turn yet already completely satisfied.

Emery lay on her back, panting, her eyes half closed. I stroked her face, overcome with adoration for the gorgeous, sexy, infuriating, intoxicating woman that I loved. Every time with her was as thrilling as the very first time, but the deep emotions between us and the history we shared meant everything just kept getting better.

Even though she drove me up the wall and around the bend, I wouldn't have had it any other way. As irritating as her bratty attitude got, I couldn't complain when it led to moments like this.

Feeling quite pleased with myself, I decided to gloat a little bit. "Well, well... Next time you'll think twice before you demand ice cream."

"Oh, really?" One tired eye flickered open. "How do you mean?"

"You acted out and you got punished."

Despite her exhaustion, a small smile played on her lips. "That's what you think?"

"Yes." I frowned, wondering what she could mean. That smile held a hint of smugness, and with every moment I watched her, it was only getting clearer.

She propped her chin in her hand, looking unnervingly self-satisfied. "Ice cream was code for sex, baby. I wanted your attention on me, not the wedding invitations."

"No." The events of the night replayed in my mind. "It can't be."

Even as I said it, my certainty was fading. Emery had a talent for getting inside my mind, guessing my next move before I'd even begun to think about it. Had I fallen into her trap once again? Given her exactly what she wanted? Searching her face, all I could see was the beauty that still took my breath away.

"You're right. I'm just kidding." She grinned at me innocently. "I wanted you to take a break. We'll finish the invitations tomorrow. Together."

I still couldn't tell if she was being genuine or not. I never quite knew true from false with my soon-to-be wife. Could never quite say what she was up to. Every time I thought there were no surprises left between us, she revealed another layer of herself, and then another.

Things could never get boring with her. She kept me on my toes, and that was why she was my perfect life partner.

Maybe she'd won this round of our game. Maybe not.

All that mattered was playing again and again with her.

ABOUT THE AUTHOR

Kim Hartfield is a queer woman who's been writing since she could pick up a pen. Her novels are sweet and steamy, and they always end with a happily ever-after. Sign up for email updates at https://sendfox.com/lp/mnleoq, find her on Facebook under Kim Hartfield, or join her Facebook group ,The Romantic Hart!

- Facebook: https://www. facebook.com/KimHartfieldAuthor/

- Facebook Group: https://www.facebook.com/ groups/1191487114538750/

SILLY GIRL

ADRIAN J. SMITH

THE WINERY

Zoe sipped at the red wine, its musky flavor lingering on the back of her tongue. She liked it, mostly. The small vials sat in front of her, and she mixed another concoction, hoping this one was better. She's been at it nearly three hours already. Her boss thought it was better if she created the star flavor for the party for who knew what reason.

Little did her boss know, Zoe wasn't an avid wine drinker and didn't fully understand the finer points of what made a good wine. But the event was supposed to be a spectacular one of the year, and Roslyn insisted on having her own flavor. Zoe didn't know why she insisted on it, but she did, so there she sat, tasting flavor after flavor.

Once she decided on one, she handed over the final selection. Heading for the door with only a slightly extra sway to her hips, she stopped short as Roslyn stood in the front of the winery.

Panic etched into Zoe's chest. "I didn't know you were coming."

"I wanted to taste." Roslyn's thin eyebrow rose, her stare intense.

Zoe couldn't ever stop the heat that rushed to her cheeks when Roslyn looked at her like that, as if she was a petulant child who needed to be put in her place. Swallowing the sudden lump in her throat, Zoe folded her hands tightly together and hoped the heat that kissed her cheeks wasn't obvious. "Oh. Um...I just finished up."

Roslyn eyed her carefully, her lips slightly parted. She may have been the top marketer at Gruszka Publishing and Zoe may have worked for her for three years as her personal assistant but that had never stopped her from daydreaming about just what those lips tasted like.

"Zoe?"

"Huh?"

"Are you drunk?" Amusement swam behind Roslyn's intense stare for a brief moment before she steeled her look again.

Heaving a sigh, Zoe flushed, embarrassment hitting her hard. She hadn't been able to hide it, and she was sure Roslyn had seen everything that flashed through her mind written across her face. "Probably."

Roslyn's voice dropped so it was barely above a whisper. She straightened her back and held herself perfectly still. Her gaze dropped from Zoe's head to her toes, slowly dragging upward again. "Silly girl."

Zoe blanched. She had no idea what to say to that. Her heart raced as she stood stiffly in front of her boss, hoping that she hadn't revealed too much. Roslyn turned to the front desk and nodded at the worker there.

"Let's taste this wine you've created." Roslyn walked confidently to the small room Zoe had just vacated after spending hours there.

Zoe followed silently, her chin tilted toward the ground in shame that she had gotten herself drunk while on the clock. They brought out the sample of wine that Zoe had mixed in a glass for Roslyn to taste in order to create the perfect flavor for the party. She sat on the edge of the table and swirled it, staring at Zoe over the edge of the glass for what felt like forever.

Zoe wasn't sure how long she would be able to stand there and not fall over. The alcohol running through her system was much stronger than she'd originally anticipated when she'd gone to leave, and it was making her head spin—or maybe that was the amused and curious look Roslyn had aimed in her direction.

"What?" Zoe asked, fear in the undertones of the word, but she was pretty sure she hid it well with a good dose of happiness. Roslyn often chided her for always being happy, but it wasn't quite true. She just used that as a cover.

Roslyn said nothing as she stared right at Zoe, lifting the wineglass to her deep red lips. Her tongue dashed out against the glass, licking up the lingering drops of the wine on the edge of it before her tongue pulled back into her mouth. Zoe had to suppress the groan that wanted to escape her lips. She clenched her jaw and fists, using the tightness of muscles and slight pain to remind herself that *this* was her boss. This was the great Roslyn Fudala, chief marketer who ran the business as if she had her finger on everything.

Zoe's breathing came in short rasps when she finally managed to relax herself, her gaze still locked on those pale blue eyes as if her entire world depended on this one woman, which she supposed it very well might. Roslyn lowered the glass and cocked her head to the side, her lips twitching in the corners before she was able to school the look.

"Is something wrong, Zoe?"

"What? Oh, no, nothing is wrong." Heat kissed her cheeks

again, and Zoe found herself unable to look away from Roslyn's intense stare.

"Are you sure?"

Zoe couldn't tell if that was fake concern, genuine concern, or amusement. She was going with the latter for now. How often was it that anyone dared to be intoxicated in front of the great Roslyn Fudala? Zoe was willing to bet never if it could be controlled.

"Zoe?" Roslyn stayed evenly in place, that gaze surreal.

Her heart raced, and her lips parted, but Zoe couldn't figure out what to say or how to answer. Was something wrong? Only this massive crush she'd had on her boss for the last three years that she had never managed to wrangle in, and with the wine in her blood and that damning look on Roslyn's face, Zoe very well may be a lesbian with her first girl crush. "Yeah?"

"Are you sure nothing's wrong?"

Shaking her head, Zoe cleared her throat. Her voice was so soft when she answered she wasn't sure Roslyn would even be able to hear her. "No, nothing is wrong."

"Hmm."

Roslyn lifted the glass to those kissable lips again and finally took a sip. The line of her throat long as the muscles moved while she swallowed. Sweat littered the small of Zoe's back and her palms as she watched Roslyn take another small sip of the blended wine. When she settled the glass onto the table and eyed Zoe up and down, Zoe was pretty sure she could come just from that look alone if given enough time.

"How drunk are you?" Roslyn asked, her tone precise as always.

Cold washed through Zoe as she blinked and tried to clear her mind from the arousal coiling in the pit of her belly. "Oh, um, well I've been here for three hours."

Roslyn eyed her again, and Zoe realized too late that she hadn't actually answered the question. Her embarrassment aside, claiming she was intoxicated was probably a good way to get out of anything stupid that was about to leave her mouth–which, if Roslyn kept looking at her like that, it likely would.

"I'm drunk. I'm really drunk," Zoe confessed, the words rushing out of her mouth before she could stop them.

Roslyn drew in a sharp breath as she grabbed the glass again and took another sip before leaving it alone and standing. She stepped in close to Zoe, bending low so her breath washed against Zoe's cheeks. "You're not supposed to swallow."

Zoe's heart raced. Heat from Roslyn's body barely touched hers because they stood so close, the line of Roslyn's arm matching with hers as they faced opposite directions. Zoe's lips parted, but she had no answers. She knew she was supposed to spit, but she'd decided to swallow a few of the flavors when they were good and had forgotten all about it in her distraction that was this gorgeous woman.

"I know," Zoe murmured.

"Then why didn't you follow the rules?" Roslyn's voice was barely above a whisper, the deep tone of her voice so seductive even though Zoe knew she hadn't meant it that way.

Tilting her chin up in a single act of defiance, Zoe looked directly into those deep, light-blue eyes. So many people thought Roslyn was cold and aloof, but after working for her for three years, Zoe knew it was exactly the opposite. She had passion underlying everything she did, deeply controlled passion.

"I don't know," Zoe answered, maintaining eye contact until she couldn't stop herself from dropping her gaze to those beautiful red lips.

Roslyn hummed again, lingering where she stood only a

breath away, her fingers gripping onto Zoe's wrist and tightening slightly before she let go and released Zoe's arm. "Come along, then. I'll drive you home. We'll send someone for your car."

THE LONELY BEDROOM

What the hell had she been thinking? Zoe groaned as she lay flat on her back in her bed, staring at her ceiling. The car ride home had been so tense, so full of idiocy on her part. She'd tried to talk about work, about the details of the party coming up, but Roslyn had headed it all off in every direction.

Turning on her side, Zoe buried her face in the pillow and clenched her eyes shut tightly. She would have to walk into the office in the morning, hungover because she definitely was drunk, and act like nothing had happened. Roslyn had spared her from as much embarrassment as possible, but still, she couldn't walk in there after today. She would be the laughingstock of everyone.

Zoe's heart wrenched. She needed to write an apology letter to Roslyn, perhaps with her resignation in it, and go from there. It was so inappropriate for her to drink while on the job. Her phone beeped, and email after email filed into it from Roslyn.

Well, that at least meant she wasn't expecting Zoe to quit or fire her, so that had to be a good sign, right? Zoe skimmed through them, looking in her declining drunken state to see what she needed to do immediately and what could wait—especially since she'd left halfway through the work day and hadn't completed everything.

The last email that came in surprised Zoe. The subject line read, *For Immediate Action*. Roslyn didn't often get that specific when she sent Zoe a list of items to do, but again, with the rest of the emails in there first, Zoe didn't think she was about to be fired for drinking on the job. Her thumb hovered over the email before she finally clicked on it while holding her breath. What punishment was she about to face? It wasn't the first time she had messed something up, but she'd never done anything this extreme before. Zoe had tried her best to maintain every boundary line possible while in the office.

For Immediate Action

I will see you in the office in the morning, eight sharp. If I discover you have done any work while you recuperate from your paid time off, there will be consequences to working off the clock.

R

Zoe read it three times over. She wasn't off the clock if it was paid time off, was it? Pulling herself to sit up, she read it a fourth time. Roslyn had never chastised her for working from home or after hours before. Nothing had happened to indicate that this was normal for them. Frequently, Roslyn would call or email or text after hours and ask Zoe to do something quickly or tell her where a file was, though rarely was she called in for something major.

Zoe read the email a fifth time, her thumb hovering over the reply button. She would be stupid to answer on a corporate email, wouldn't she? Yet, she wanted to. She wanted to tell Roslyn she was fine and could work from home on certain projects, nothing that would go out until she was sober enough to double-check her work, but she'd sobered a bit since Roslyn had brought her back to her small apartment.

What was she supposed to even say back that wouldn't be considered inappropriate? Zoe pushed her thumb against the reply button on her phone and stared at the blank email. In an instant, she was typing quickly.

RE: *For Immediate Action*

Ms. Fudala,

I don't believe PTO means I am off the clock.

Sincerely,
Zoe

She hit send before she could chicken out and settled the phone down onto her chest. A smile lingered on her lips. She'd never been so forward with Roslyn before, never pushed back on the limits she had set. Perhaps the alcohol still lingering in her blood stream was giving her the voice she always wanted.

Arousal coiled through her again as she imagined the look on Roslyn's face when she read Zoe's response. She wasn't sure when it happened, but she found her hand pressed between her legs, smoothly running her fingers over herself, using the friction of her cotton panties to tease. It had been a long time since she'd touched herself while thinking of Roslyn. After the first few times, she had stopped, needing to have more space between them instead of less, and when she did this, she couldn't stop thinking about Roslyn touching her instead.

Zoe drew in a sharp breath as she eased one finger under the edge of her underwear and brushed the pad against her swollen lips. The moan from her lips was light. Her eyelids fluttered shut at the barest touch, and she wished it was Roslyn's hand instead of hers. Still, this was as good as she would ever get from her boss, so she would take what she was given.

As soon as she made the decision, Zoe went all in. She lifted her hips and shoved her sleep shorts to the bottom of the bed along with her panties. Sitting up, she stripped off the tank top she'd changed into when she'd come home and dropped it to the side of the bed.

"In for a penny," Zoe murmured as she laid back on the bed and closed her eyes.

She started slowly, sliding one finger in a circle around her clit before gently rubbing back and forth. She relaxed into the moment, using the image of Roslyn sitting on that table, the direct look, the amusement behind the gaze. Zoe was probably just making up that last bit, but she would roll with it for now.

Sighing, Zoe pressed a little harder and slid two fingers inside herself. She'd done this so many times in the last few years that she knew the fastest way to bring herself up. With her thumb moving, Zoe kept her eyes closed and imagined Roslyn as the one between her legs.

Normally she hated thinking of other people, but clearly with enough alcohol in her system in the middle of the day, her brain wasn't thinking clearly. Zoe bucked her hips suddenly, her voice echoing throughout her room.

"Oh, yeah, that feels good." She kept her eyes clenched shut, doing everything solely by feel as she continued to pleasure herself. It would take months for her to pull back from this while working with Roslyn in the office, but at the same time, Zoe couldn't stop. She needed it.

Her lips parted as another wave of pleasure rolled through her. The alcohol might be impeding her ability to come as quickly as she wanted, but she would stick it through until she crested through at least one orgasm. She was just about to hit that first edge of the cliff when there was no turning back, when her phone vibrated loudly against the mattress.

Cursing, Zoe reached for it and grabbed the phone hard. She tensed when she saw Roslyn's name on the screen. She answered before she missed the call, never wanting to miss a call from the queen.

"Ros–Ms. Fudala, what can I help you with?" Zoe was out of breath, her heart racing and her head pounding as she tried to decide what to do and say next. She'd been caught red-handed, her fingers still inside her, her thumb still on her clit, and somehow, she had to focus on that sultry voice.

"Zoe," Roslyn responded. "I'm calling about your email."

Zoe whimpered. Of all things for Roslyn to call about, this was the last thing she expected. She knew she'd been petulant in her response, but she couldn't believe Roslyn would call over this. "Wh-what about it?"

Why did she sound so out of breath? Her heart picked up speed, and she was sure Roslyn would know what she had been up to. She shouldn't have answered. She knew she couldn't hold her tongue when alcohol was involved, and this was only going to make it worse.

"I've put you in for a sick day. Take it. We can survive half a day without you."

Zoe sighed, pushing her thumb into her clit harder. Roslyn's tone was always so precise, her words exact. Zoe swallowed and bit her lip as her eyes fluttered shut. "Right. I'll take the rest of the day."

"Good." Roslyn sounded pleased.

Zoe wasn't sure what to say beyond hanging up. "Is that everything?"

"Yes. I'll see you in the morning, and I expect you to be at your best."

"Right. See you tomorrow." Zoe clenched her jaw to hold back the moan. Was she actually doing this? She sped up her fingers, the last note of Roslyn's voice echoing in her mind. She put her phone next to her and dragged in a refreshing breath of air.

This time she groaned loudly, her hips rising from the mattress as she brought herself right back up to that first edge. Her breathing came in gasps as she flicked her thumb hard over her clit, her body jerking in response. She grunted as pleasure pooled between her legs, faster than she could breathe, as if stacking every nerve ending on fire together was a brilliant idea, but it was. *God, it was.*

Zoe whimpered, her voice ringing in her ears as she pushed her way through her orgasm and kept her thumb moving in slow circles to drag it out entirely. As she relaxed onto the bed, she breathed a sigh of relief. It may have been unorthodox, but she was glad she'd done it. Reaching for her phone, she went to check the emails, except — Roslyn was still on the line.

No.

She had ended the call, hadn't she?

"Fuck." Zoe hit the big red button, triple checked to make sure the call was ended and buried her face in her pillow dominated by embarrassment. She was done for. She would most certainly be fired now. "Fuck."

THE WALK OF SHAME

Zoe dragged herself to work at seven-forty-five in the morning. She had spent the entire night preparing herself for the explanation of a lifetime, for begging to be spared her job, for groveling at Roslyn's feet.

Except when she got to the office, Roslyn wasn't in yet. She knew she was early, but more often than not, Roslyn was the first to arrive. She was there when Zoe got there and she was there when Zoe left. Sitting at her desk, awkwardly, Zoe started in on her morning routine, needing to do something otherwise she would worry herself to death.

She was halfway through the email list from the previous day when Roslyn finally stepped into the office. She nodded once at Zoe and immediately went into her main office, the door shutting as she disappeared inside. Zoe's heart was in her throat, and she hadn't even managed to get out a "Morning, Ms. Fudala" like she did every day. She'd been stunned into silence.

Zoe stayed seated, unsure of what to do next. Maybe if they just didn't talk about it, then it didn't really happen. Zoe scoffed. That was a bunch of bologna if she knew it. Of course it had happened, not only had she masturbated while on a work call, but a call with her boss, with her boss who she'd had a massive crush on for the last three years they had worked together, three years where she had managed to maintain absolute professionalism.

Groaning, Zoe took a deep breath and focused her mind on her work. She would wait until Roslyn came out to speak with her. Checking Roslyn's schedule, Zoe noted she had been late to a video meeting, which was certainly why she hadn't said anything when she came in. That put Zoe's heart at ease.

Puttering away at more work, Zoe did her best to forget the incident the other night. It was close to lunch before Roslyn emerged from the interior office and leaned against the door frame, her legs crossed, and her gaze directly on Zoe as she sat at the desk deep in work. Zoe caught sight of her and stopped instantly, fear ratcheting up in her chest again.

"Ms. Fudala, did you need something?"

That sly smile Zoe swore she saw the day before was back, before it was immediately masked by something else, something she couldn't read other than Roslyn's normal countenance. "I need the final edits on the Granular file. They're insisting I go through them."

"Right, I'll get hold of it and get it to you right away."

Roslyn stayed put, not moving and staring Zoe down.

"Was that all you needed?" Zoe's heart was in her throat again. She hated being in this position, not knowing what Roslyn was thinking, if this was going to be the end of her career, or if they were even going to speak of it.

Roslyn's lips pressed together tightly, pursing as she pushed off the wall and took careful, precise steps toward her. Zoe couldn't breathe. She'd been waiting for this moment, when everything would come tumbling out over her own stupidity.

Roslyn leaned over the desk, her palm planted on the sleek

wood. She reached toward her belly, Zoe's eyes riveted to every movement she made, and she pulled the single button on her jacket to release it. Zoe's breath caught, and she had to force herself to drag her gaze upward to Roslyn's face, realizing far too late that she had been looking elsewhere.

"We do need to talk at some point."

Zoe held her breath. "Okay?"

"About yesterday."

She was being so vague. About being drunk while on the job? About masturbating to images of her boss, to the sound of her boss telling her what to do in her mind? About—

"Focus, Zoe."

"Yes, Ms. Fudala." Zoe flushed, embarrassment slamming down on her again only this time for something else entirely.

"I don't have time to talk today."

"Do you want me to schedule it in?"

Roslyn hummed, shifting so she was leaning forward on the desk even more, close enough that Zoe could move upward slightly and they could kiss. Though she would never do that. She could never—

"Zoe." Roslyn firmly chastised her for losing her train of thought again.

"Yes, sorry, Ms. Fudala. I'm focusing."

"Are you?" Roslyn raised an eyebrow and drew in a deep breath, her breasts pushing against the tight fabric of her blouse. "I think we can find time to fit in the conversation around my schedule. Don't you?"

"Yes, Ms. Fudala, whatever you think needs to happen."

"Right. The Granular fie?"

"On it." Zoe couldn't drag her eyes away from Roslyn as she straightened her back, the flaps of her jacket falling to the sides. Roslyn dragged it off, over her shoulders, and folded it over her arm. Zoe swallowed hard, the snake of arousal that had bitten her last night coming back to haunt her as she openly roved her gaze over Roslyn's body.

Roslyn cleared her throat, and Zoe immediately looked at her computer and typed out the end of the email she had been about ready to send when Roslyn had come to speak with her. Eventually Roslyn turned and walked back to her office, the lines of her body exact as she walked.

Zoe swore she heard her mutter *silly girl* as she shut the door and went back to work.

Blowing out a breath of relief, Zoe grabbed the office phone and put a call down for the Granular file to be delivered immediately.

THE PARTY

Everything was perfect, though Zoe expected nothing less. They had spent months planning this party for the release of what Roslyn thought was going to be the next big book series out there. They invited all the big names, all the board members, everyone they could possibly think of.

Zoe was happy to see it all come to fruition, finally. She'd spent countless hours answering phone calls and emails to get everything done, doing most of the grunt work in the meantime. Roslyn could have used someone else to plan the party, but she'd taken on this series as her pet project and wanted her hand in everything. Hence the wine.

Zoe stared at a waitress with a tray, wine glasses on top of it as she moved around the vast room and distributed it. Zoe's stomach clenched at the memory of what that wine held. Not just her first stupid mistake of getting drunk, but her second one of masturbating while thinking of her boss and not double-checking that the phone call was ended.

"Are you going to have some?" Roslyn's deep voice reverberated in her ear.

Zoe tensed, turning slowly to find Roslyn right over her shoulder and a wine glass in hand. Thankfully, only one. "I think I've had enough of that wine to last me a lifetime."

Roslyn chuckled lightly. It had been nearly a month since that fateful day, and they had never had their little chat about what had happened. Zoe kept waiting for it, any time Roslyn called her into her office, any time there was an email set up saying they needed to go over some things but no details were specified. Yet, there had been nothing.

"Perhaps sticking to water would best." Roslyn brought the glass to her lips and took a small sip.

Zoe swore she placed feather light touches against her back, but she had to be making it up. Roslyn had never touched her like that. "Yes, I think that would be wise. At least while I'm working."

Roslyn's gaze became amused before she immediately masked it again. "It's a party, Zoe. At least learn to enjoy yourself a little."

Zoe wasn't sure how to respond to that. While yes, she wanted to enjoy herself, she was at work, and she was there for a purpose. If she wasn't Roslyn's personal assistant, she was pretty sure she would have never been invited to something this rich. Turning so they were facing each other, Zoe had to hold back her groan. She should have stayed put.

Roslyn was dressed impeccably, classically. The black material smoothed over her pale skin as it draped around her curves. A lump formed in Zoe's throat as she lost the ability to form all words. Her mouth was dry. One of Roslyn's shoulders was bare while the other covered, but skin was revealed just below. Zoe would love to trace her tongue right along that line, across the top of her breasts, under the hem of the material.

She clenched her jaw shut tightly, dropping her gaze to the slit, high on Roslyn's thigh, high enough that she could easily reach in and—fuck, she had to stop that train of thought. Licking her lips from her suddenly parched mouth, Zoe deliberately raised her eyes to see exactly what Roslyn was thinking.

"Wine?" Roslyn looked...amused?

Surely she didn't find this entertaining. Zoe took the proffered glass and put it to her lips, sipping the wine she had spent hours creating, so it was the perfect flavor for the night. It hit the back of her throat, and she nearly sputtered at the intense stare Roslyn gave her.

"We never did have that chat, did we?" Roslyn's voice was so quiet, Zoe wasn't sure she'd heard correctly.

"What chat?" Zoe asked, holding the glass tightly between her fingers until Roslyn took it from her grasp.

"The one about the winery and what happened...after."

Zoe's stomach clenched hard. Roslyn stepped in closer, lowering her tones so it was just above a whisper as she leaned in and put her lips right next to Zoe's ear.

"About your email and our...little...phone call."

Oh fuck, she was done for. Zoe listed forward, and Roslyn put a hand on her arm to steady her. Her fingers were so warm, so firm. Zoe whimpered at just the thought of what she could use them for.

"Don't be afraid," Roslyn dropped her voice even lower. Zoe had to lean in to hear her, pressing against Roslyn's side as they stood together. "I promise our little chat will be pleasant."

The way she said the last word sent a shiver down Zoe's spine, ending right between her legs. Zoe had to press her thighs together at the intrusive thoughts that hit her brain. Again, Roslyn's fingers were at her back, pressing firmly into the bare skin where her dress didn't touch.

"I'm looking forward to seeing what explanation you have to offer." Without another word, Roslyn stepped away with her wineglass in her hand. She moved to talk to one of the board members, as if nothing had been exchanged between them.

Zoe tried to shake the thought from her head because Roslyn had confirmed nothing other than the fact she had known exactly what Zoe was doing that night. *Damn it.* She had really hoped Roslyn had been so distracted by work that she hadn't noticed the call hadn't ended. Embarrassment flooded into her again, her cheeks heating as a waiter walked by her. Zoe requested a water, and when the waiter returned, she was glad for the cold liquid flowing through her body.

She couldn't take her eyes off Roslyn the entire night. The woman seemed to flirt with everyone, her eyes lighting up as she moved from person to person, the conversation flowing from her perfectly. Zoe had seen her in this environment before, but she'd never paid close enough attention to see the underlying emotions flashing through Roslyn's gaze–the annoyance, the temper, the true genuine friendship.

Zoe took in every aspect, stilling when Roslyn looked across at her, their gazes locking. Roslyn raised an eyebrow, lips curling upward into a seductive smile. It lasted only a brief second before Roslyn's attention was pulled back to the two people in front of her. Zoe breathed out a sigh of relief and stepped away from the ballroom.

She needed some fresh air. They had rented the ballroom in one of the nicer hotels in town, a place their publishing company often did business with. Zoe set her glass on a table as she stepped out into the hallway and made her way toward one of the balconies. They were on the fifth floor, and outside the city ran circles around them. Everything inside had stopped for fun, for celebration, for a moment to be together.

Leaning over the railing, Zoe dragged in a deep breath. She had to stop reading into so much between her and Roslyn. It was all in her head–there was nothing between them. She'd spent too many nights fantasizing about what they might to do together, but that's all it was, fantasy.

"I hope you're not thinking of jumping."

Zoe stiffened, straightening her back as she spun around to find Roslyn eyeing her up and down. That dress was still gorgeous on her, nothing that would ever suit Zoe and her tastes. Roslyn's hair was done up, twisted into a simple bun near the top of her head, her makeup painted beautifully so her eyes seemed bigger, her features more exotic.

"No, not planning on jumping."

"Couldn't have that." Roslyn stepped in close, her fingers flitting over Zoe's arm.

They had never really touched before, or if they did, it was extremely rare. Zoe had taken great pains to maintain a professional distance between the two of them. She also had no idea what to say.

"I hope..." Roslyn stopped, moving her gaze from Zoe to the city below them. "Is this where you'd like to talk?"

"Talk about what, exactly?" Zoe looked Roslyn over carefully, trying to read every intonation.

Roslyn hummed, but instead of a noncommittal answer like it normally was, this held something in it. Zoe stepped in closer, taking a firm risk in reaching out and covering Roslyn's fingers with her own.

"Are you firing me?"

"What? No." Roslyn raised her gaze. "Why would you think that?"

"B-because of what happened at the winery." *And after...* she wanted to say but didn't.

"Silly girl," Roslyn whispered as if this time it was a term of endearment. "I'm not firing you."

"Oh good." Relief flooded through Zoe, and she let go of

Roslyn's hands, only to have Roslyn grip her fingers. "What's wrong?"

"Stop asking me that," Zoe muttered.

Confusion clouded Roslyn's eyes, and Zoe had to step away from her, putting space between them. Her heart thundered as she leaned over the railing, trying to push Roslyn from her mind, but it was so hard with her standing right there, right next to her, the heat from her body warming the chill that had taken over.

"Talk to me, Zoe."

"Are you going to fire me?" Zoe lifted her chin up defiantly. "Because I love my job, Ms. Fudala. I love working for you and the work that we do, and I don't want to lose my job."

Roslyn frowned but stayed stoically still. "Why do you think you deserve to be fired?"

That was a question she hadn't been expecting. "Because of the winery."

"Because you drank while on the job?" Roslyn pressed her hand to Zoe's back, encouraging Zoe to stand up straight and turn so they could look at each other. "We're drinking on the job tonight."

"Not because of that." Zoe's voice was so quiet, she wasn't even sure Roslyn had heard her. In fact, she would be happier if she hadn't. With no alcohol in her system as an excuse, she couldn't easily get out of this confession if she were to make it.

Roslyn's eyes lit up, and her lips curled seductively. Leaning in, she pressed her mouth to Zoe's ear and squeezed her fingers tightly. "Do you know how many women and men are attracted to me?"

Zoe's stomach plummeted. She hadn't wanted the conversation to turn this direction, and with what Roslyn had just said, she knew exactly where it was going. She was no one. She was a personal assistant to a high-powered woman and she couldn't compare to anyone Roslyn could have if she so much as said the word.

"But all of them want something from me." Roslyn wrapped her arm around Zoe's side, holding them close together. "You have never once asked for anything from me. You are unique in that, silly girl."

Zoe's heart fluttered. But again, she was at a loss for words.

"I thought your little crush had disappeared over the last few years, but recently, I've discovered it's quite the opposite."

Her heart sank. Roslyn's words were so pointed. Zoe had thought she'd hidden it well for all these years, but she hadn't. "I don't know what you mean."

Roslyn chuckled, all knowing. "Don't start denying it now."

"I'm not." Zoe tilted into Roslyn until her lips pressed delicately against her chin. She let out a shuddering breath and closed her eyes, daring herself to dream. This could be it, couldn't it? She wasn't making all this up.

"Will you come with me?" Roslyn loosened her grasp and slid away to look into Zoe's eyes.

Zoe swallowed hard, her heart racing. She knew exactly what she was agreeing to, and she wanted nothing else. "Yes."

THE SEDUCTION

They moved swiftly through the hallways until they reached the elevator. Zoe's heart was in her throat as soon as they were inside and Roslyn pressed a button for the thirty-second floor. Zoe stood still. Roslyn's fingers curled around hers as they stood at the door in absolute silence. She knew her boss wasn't someone who spoke in abundance. For as much as she read, she was rather quiet. But when she did say something, everyone in the room listened.

"Where are we going?" Zoe asked.

Roslyn glanced at Zoe. "To my room. I rented it when I knew tonight was going to be late and I didn't want to have to travel home exhausted."

"You rented a room?" Zoe looked at the buttons as they moved from one floor to the next.

Bringing Zoe's hand up to her lips, Roslyn pressed a delicate kiss against Zoe's knuckles. "Yes. I've been doing this for years. Makes it easier in the morning."

"How did I not know that?" Zoe was stumped. She thought

she'd known everything about Roslyn, but this was something else entirely. Staring forward, she was surprised when Roslyn lifted her chin with one finger and pressed their lips together.

Heat seared through her body. Every place they touched, screaming for more. This was better than anything Zoe could have imagined. She moved her free hand up, curling it around the back of Roslyn's neck and holding her in place as she deepened the kiss.

Roslyn pushed her against the door to the elevator, skimming her hand down Zoe's chest, over her breasts, and back up again to curl delicately around the front of her neck. Zoe let loose. She'd been dreaming of this moment for years, and it was everything she had imagined and more. Roslyn was fire underneath everything.

Smashed between her hot boss and the cold elevator doors, Zoe let herself only feel. Their bodies were pressed tightly together, her hand at the back of Roslyn's neck tightening to keep her right where Zoe wanted her. Zoe bucked her hips, needing Roslyn to touch her everywhere.

"Oh God," Zoe muttered, tossing her head back into the door as Roslyn trailed kisses down her neck. She had never imagined this night would move in this direction. Roslyn chuckled low, her voice reverberating through Zoe's chest causing her nipples to harden. She would do anything for this woman. She'd never had any doubt of that.

The elevator stopped, and Zoe waited for Roslyn to move away, but she didn't. She nipped at Zoe's collarbone, brushed fingers over her breasts again, and pecked her lips quickly. "My room."

Zoe whined. Roslyn led the way as they moved swiftly from the elevator to the door. She pressed the code into the keypad and opened it as soon as the lock beeped. In seconds, they were inside, and Zoe found herself plastered between the door and Roslyn again. This time, their kisses were furious.

She wanted to speak. She wanted to say what she was feeling and thinking, but she worried that to utter even one word would ruin the moment and pull them out of it–that it wasn't what Roslyn wanted. Zoe held Roslyn close, her hands on each side of her face. In an instant, she pushed off the door and flipped them around.

Roslyn grinned, that saucy smile immediate. Zoe filed that moment away to remember the next time she needed to use her hand, because surely this was only going to happen once. She did what she had wanted to do all night, and she found the slit in Roslyn's dress, high up on her thigh and wove her hand under it.

"Touch me," Roslyn murmured, her eyes half-lidded as she rested her shoulders against the door and let Zoe have access to every part of her body. "I'm yours."

Zoe's heart shattered. This was more than a quick fuck for her, but she would take everything Roslyn offered. Like she did every day, she would do anything Roslyn asked of her. She nipped down Roslyn's neck, sliding her tongue under the fabric of her dress and across the tops of her breasts. She tasted just as good as Zoe had imagined.

"Take me already." Roslyn looked down at her, cool blue eyes boring directly into Zoe's soul.

"Yeah," Zoe whispered, sliding her hand up Roslyn's thigh. She didn't need to be told three times. She fumbled at first, trying to find the best way to slide her fingers, to rub and move.

Roslyn groaned, her voice echoing into the room beyond them. Zoe drew in a deep breath to steady her hand and pressed her lips to Roslyn's neck again. She needed to distract not only Roslyn, but herself from her own trepidation.

"Fuck me," Roslyn murmured. "I need you to touch me."

She'd been told enough. Zoe pushed aside the thong and slid two fingers inside, using Roslyn's own moisture against her clit as she rubbed circles. *Fuck, she was soaked.* The cotton of the thong was wet against the back of her hand as she began a slow thrust. Roslyn rocked her hips, no doubt increasing the friction between them.

Zoe matched her rhythm. This woman was a goddess in human form. Roslyn's cheeks flushed as pleasure poured into her. Zoe loved seeing every change in her, the relaxed jaw, the half-lidded eyes, the red running over her chest and neck. Leaning in, Zoe nipped at Roslyn's neck and bit hard enough to leave a mark.

Roslyn whined. The noise sent shivers through Zoe. She could come just from listening to Roslyn's noises. She bit again, changing the angle of her wrist and the pressure of her thumb to make it slightly harder than before.

"That's it," Roslyn murmured, digging her fingers into Zoe's hair and holding her tightly. "Don't stop. It feels so good."

Zoe dashed her tongue against Roslyn's salty neck, then scraped her teeth down until she ran into the damn dress again. It might have been fun to play with for a brief second, but Zoe would much rather have her naked.

"Just a little bit longer." Roslyn's voice was breathy, and she struggled to form the words.

Zoe did exactly as she asked. She kept the pace, she kept the pressure, and she made sure Roslyn came first.

Roslyn clenched hard against Zoe's fingers, her entire body tightening as she gripped Zoe and held her in her arms. She grunted lightly, her breathing uneven. Satisfied she had done what was asked of her, Zoe removed her hand and licked her fingers. Roslyn's flavor burst on her tongue, and she was determined it would be something she would never forget. If this was all she got, it was worth it.

Without another moment, Roslyn gripped Zoe by the back of the head and pressed their mouths together. In seconds, she had the back of Zoe's dress undone and slid it down her body to land in a pool of fabric on the floor. Roslyn stepped forward, making Zoe step backward. Her bra was next.

Her back collided with the wall, and Roslyn's mouth was on her breasts, circling her nipple with her tongue before flicking it hard. Zoe dug her fingers into Roslyn's dark luscious hair, pulling it out of the damnable bun she'd had it in all night. Roslyn moved down her body to her belly before trailing her way back up and kissing Zoe so hard she lost all sense of time and space.

"Touch yourself. I need a minute," Roslyn whispered into Zoe's ear, stepping away. She eyed Zoe pointedly until Zoe moved her panties down to her thighs and plunged the fingers she'd just used in Roslyn into her own body. "Absolutely perfect. Watch yourself in the mirror."

Zoe turned her chin toward the large floor-to-ceiling mirror across from her. She'd never done this before, but it was the most erotic thing she had experienced to date. Roslyn disappeared into the bathroom, and when she came out, she was completely bare. Her lips curled at the sight of Zoe still fingering herself.

"I think we should take these off." She stepped in front of Zoe and pulled her panties the rest of the way off.

Instead of standing up like Zoe had thought she would, Roslyn stayed on the floor, her knees pressing into the carpet as she spread Zoe's legs a little wider. Her mouth was on Zoe instantly. Crying out in surprise, Zoe pushed against the wall to hold herself up and couldn't stop staring at Roslyn's back in the mirror, her head between Zoe's legs as she took deep breaths and put all that concentration she had into one thing. *Zoe.*

Biting her tongue to hold back her groan, Zoe pressed her

palms flat against the wall until she had to hold on to Roslyn to keep herself upright. She clenched her eyes tightly, trying to rid her brain of the powerful woman between her legs. It made her too weak in her knees. Zoe took in shallow breaths, her hips jerking as she got even closer to the precipice of her orgasm.

She tried to speak, tried to say anything that would tell Roslyn exactly what she was feeling or needed, but she couldn't form a single word. Roslyn's fingers dug into her hips to hold her steady, and she was pretty sure she was going to fall over without the added stability. It felt amazing, so good, so beyond what any stupid imagination and her own hand could do.

Sweat riddled along her skin, her chest covered in red splotches. Zoe opened her eyes and stared down at Roslyn, crashing through her orgasm unexpectedly. She jerked, she clenched her fingers tightly. She held on for dear life as Roslyn continued to suck and tease.

"Enough," Zoe breathed out, unable to form any other word.

Roslyn kissed the inside of Zoe's thigh, nipping her tender flesh. "Talk to me, Zoe."

She shook her head, unable to speak. No matter what she tried, she couldn't even come up with one damn single word.

"Zoe," Roslyn cooed, standing right next to her and running soothing hands over her arms and fingers over her cheeks. "Talk to me."

Shaking her head again, Zoe pried her eyes open and stared directly into those blue eyes, ones she had dreamed about for years. This couldn't be real, could it? Pulling Roslyn in closer, Zoe took her mouth in a gentle kiss. She tried to make it all physical, but she couldn't. She wanted more than just that even if she knew it wasn't going to be more. Roslyn didn't have relationships. The closest Zoe had seen in three years to a relationship was a repeated fling.

Zoe took a step, pushing away from the wall and steering Roslyn toward the bed. They walked like that, hands teasing, mouths connected, until Roslyn fell back. Zoe kept her mouth closed as she climbed onto the mattress and kissed her way down Roslyn's chest and stomach.

"Zoe, please."

She had no idea what Roslyn was asking for. It could be so many things. She fingered Roslyn's clit again while her tongue was occupied with drawing designs on her smooth skin.

"Talk to me," Roslyn murmured, but her hips moved upward in an invitation for Zoe to go closer.

Listening to the physical call, Zoe covered Roslyn with her mouth. The flavor she'd only gotten a taste of before blossomed on her tongue. She drew in deep breaths as she pulled Roslyn up for a second orgasm of the night. If they could stay in that position all night, giving each other pleasure, taking what they wanted, Zoe would be a happy woman, but she would make sure she was gone by morning.

Roslyn gripped her hair tightly, tugging hard as her muscles clamped down. Zoe continued to lick until Roslyn gasped for air and turned on her side to stop it. Wiping her face with the back of her hand, Zoe sat on the edge of the bed and looked Roslyn over. She was even more beautiful now than before, if that was even possible. Her hair was a mess, strands pulled from the bun and falling across the sheets, her eyelids half-closed from sleep, and her skin riddled with goosebumps from the aftermath of sex.

"Come here," Roslyn said, her voice rough.

Zoe complied, but still said nothing. She climbed into Roslyn's arms, turning so her back was against Roslyn's front. She couldn't look at her. She would be too embarrassed to think this would never happen again. Her heart ached, but she didn't regret it for one moment. Roslyn traced fingers down her side, over her hip, and to her thigh.

"Talk to me, Zoe. I need to know what you're thinking."

She almost whimpered. Zoe couldn't think of anything to say. Closing her eyes, she feigned sleep.

THE DESK

Zoe hadn't seen Roslyn in two days. The entire weekend, all she had done was dream about their one night together and the way she had snuck out in the middle of it when she was sure Roslyn was deep asleep. When she came into the office that morning, Roslyn was already at her desk, the lights on in her office, and she was bent over it, deep in work. Swallowing hard, Zoe slipped her bag into her bottom drawer and sat down. She turned on her computer and got to work.

It was hours before Roslyn stepped out of her office, crossing her arms as she leaned against the door frame and staring directly at Zoe as if she had all the time in the world to stand there and wait. Zoe bit the inside of her cheek, still at a complete loss for words.

"I knew I was right about you," Roslyn stated, her voice firm with an edge to it that she couldn't quite place.

Zoe's stomach dropped. "Right about what, Ms. Fudala?"

Roslyn stayed still one moment too long, and Zoe wondered what she had done to make her mad this time. She'd avoided work all weekend. She'd barely even checked her emails and text messages, not that she had gotten any from Roslyn in the meantime.

In silence, Roslyn stood up straight and strode to the main door, shutting it before facing Zoe down with a stern look. "I told you one thing on Friday."

Zoe wanted to ask what that was, but she feared the repercussions. Her heart thumped wildly as Roslyn stepped closer to her, the lines of her legs shifting the pencil skirt as she moved, and Zoe had to work too damn hard to lift her gaze back to those all-seeing blue eyes.

"That's it right there, isn't it?"

Roslyn sounded as though she'd figured it out. Whatever it was, Zoe had no idea, but she wasn't about to reveal any more than she had to. She was going to keep silent for as long as possible.

"Did you know I spent all weekend thinking about Friday?"

Roslyn slid onto the edge of Zoe's desk, crossing her legs so her skirt hiked up high, revealing small circular bruises on the inside of one of her thighs. A thrill ran through Zoe at the thought that she'd caused those. Immediately, she looked at Roslyn's neck to see if there were bite marks there, but she didn't find any. Roslyn bent down, the open line of her button-up shirt revealing the edge of her beige bra as she moved.

"Oh yes, they're there," Roslyn accused quietly. "I had to spend quite a bit of time putting concealer on them this morning."

Zoe drew in a sharp breath, her lips parting as if she was going to say something, but words still failed her. Tentatively, Zoe reached out and ran her fingers along Roslyn's smooth skin, across the bruises she had left there days ago. They looked beautiful, covering Roslyn's leg as though Roslyn really was hers. Except she didn't own her. It had been one night together and nothing more.

Pulling her hand away, Zoe squared her shoulders and sat up straight in her chair. "I have work to do, Ms. Fudala."

Roslyn grinned, satisfaction settling into her look as she leaned in even closer, putting her hand on top of Zoe's. "I do believe I'm your boss."

"Y-yes," Zoe stuttered, not moving.

"Which means I get to decide what you do when."

She clenched her jaw and shook her head. "No, Ms. Fudala. I do what needs done for you, to make your job easier and smoother."

"Yes, I would like for that to happen." Roslyn moved in closer, nipping Zoe's earlobe and pulling. "And I would like it if you would talk to me."

"There's nothing to talk about," Zoe whispered, turning her cheek so her face brushed against Roslyn's.

Confusion riddled Roslyn's eyes as she pulled away. "I thought this was something you wanted."

"It was."

Roslyn jerked her head sharply to the side. "It was or it *is*?"

Zoe's lips parted, but again it seemed as if she had no answer. Whatever they were doing couldn't go anywhere, could it? "I was drunk when you called me that day."

"I know," Roslyn whispered, a smile playing at her lips. "And it is likely one of the most interesting phone calls I have ever had with you."

"It won't happen again. I'm sorry it did the first time."

"I'm not." Roslyn took Zoe's hand and pressed it to her warm thigh. "It's what led to Friday night."

Zoe couldn't deny that, and she was even more distracted than before. Roslyn reached up and pulled the button on her shirt, revealing even more of the lace beige bra she wore. Zoe flicked her gaze up to Roslyn's eyes. "What are you doing?"

"Exactly what I've wanted for years."

"Years?" Zoe choked out.

"Mmhmm." Roslyn pulled another button. "Unless, of course you want me to stop."

"No," Zoe murmured, completely entranced by the woman in front of her. Raising her hand, she reached into Roslyn's shirt and cupped her breast, flicking her thumb over the hard nub of her nipple.

"Silly girl," Roslyn whispered as she bent down again, parting her legs so Zoe could slide right between them in her chair. "Why would you think after Friday that I wouldn't be completely addicted to your touch?"

"Oh God," Zoe muttered just before Roslyn took her mouth. She couldn't say no. She could never say no to this woman. She held so much power, so much control, that everything she said was exactly what the world needed to do in order to be graced with her presence.

"Perfect," Roslyn mumbled as she kissed along Zoe's jawline and slid off the edge of the desk. Once again, she was on her knees, her back to the desk as their mouths connected. Zoe whined, needing more of this woman, needing more touches.

Roslyn pressed her palms to Zoe's knees and pushed the skirt she wore up. Zoe lifted her butt off the chair so that Roslyn would have more access. She was already wet, dripping. One look from this woman could do that to her, and it hadn't been something she ever wanted to give up.

Pressing kisses over Zoe's clothes, Roslyn bent her head to tease the supple flesh at Zoe's legs, much the way she had done for Roslyn on Friday. Whimpering, Zoe shifted in her chair, unable to stay still. She was about to cry out when Roslyn bit particularly hard, but the door to the offices opened, and she jerked with a start, pushing her chair into her desk to cover the fact that Roslyn was still seated on her knees between her legs.

"Mr. Gruszka." Surprise was in her voice, but there was no way for her to cover it up. Thankfully, Roslyn stopped touching her and stilled. Zoe's heart raced as she stared at the middle-aged man with salt-and-pepper hair. "What can I do for you?"

"I need to speak with Roslyn."

"She's...uh...not in her office right now." It wasn't a complete lie, but it was the best she could do at the moment.

Mr. Gruszka frowned and glanced at Roslyn's open office door with the light still on. "I can wait."

"She's with a client. I'm sorry, but it's going to be a bit before she gets back." Zoe clenched her jaw, her knee slamming into the top of her desk when Roslyn's thin fingers worked up straight between her legs.

He eyed Zoe suspiciously. "She didn't have anything on her calendar."

"I must have forgotten to put it in, but it was a last-minute meeting." Zoe tried to give him a smile to assuage any ruffled feathers, but she worried it came out more as a grimace when Roslyn pressed one finger deep inside her, curling it up.

She had to swallow back a moan when Roslyn pushed her knees apart, the heat from her mouth covering Zoe's clit. Her cheeks flushed hard, and Mr. Gruszka leaned over her desk and pointed at the calendar she had laid out on the top. "I need to speak with her as soon as possible. When is she back?"

"Oh...um..." Zoe dragged the calendar closer to her and stared at it, having to refocus her eyes twice in order to read her own handwriting on it. "She should be back in a few hours and have some time around three this afternoon."

"I'll see her then." He raised an eyebrow at her. "Are you all right? Not sick?"

"No," Zoe squeaked when Roslyn hit a particularly plea-surable rhythm. "I think I'm still tired from the party this week-end. Organizing that was a feat."

"It was." He pursed his lips at her. "But it was an excellent party. I hope Roslyn let you enjoy it."

"She did." Zoe dragged in a deep breath. "Trust me, she did."

He nodded at the calendar. "Pencil me in."

"Will do." She gasped on the last word, Roslyn pushing hard into her clit. Zoe held herself as still as possible until he got to the office door, giving him the best smile she could under the circumstances. "Will you shut it, please?"

Mr. Gruszka gave her an odd look, but complied with her request. Zoe wished she had a moment to get up and lock it, but she was pretty sure Roslyn wasn't going to give her a chance. She didn't even have a moment to pull her chair away as Roslyn flicked her tongue hard against her clit.

Zoe groaned, gripping the edge of her desk to hold herself steady while Roslyn fucked her harder than she had ever dreamed. Her entire body heated, tingles running through every fucking nerve she had, and in seconds she was crashing through an orgasm that left her head reeling.

As she came back to herself, she eased the chair away only to find Roslyn grinning like an idiot under the desk. She climbed out, but when Zoe went to drag her skirt down, Roslyn stopped her by leaning in and capturing her lips in a passionate kiss. Their tongues tangled fiercely, as if battling for control, but Zoe knew Roslyn would win any battle they had. She moaned again when Roslyn bit her lower lip, sucking it hard enough that Zoe was sure it would be red and swollen.

"You are such a good pet. I think I'll keep you," Roslyn murmured, kissing her hard again.

Zoe forgot all about the unlocked door, about the fact she

was at work in the middle of the day with her boss between her legs, about the fact that this wasn't supposed to happen again. She couldn't have asked for it any other way. As soon as Roslyn released her, Zoe looked deep into those pale blue eyes.

"What now?" Zoe whispered.

The wicked grin on Roslyn's mouth was enough to scare her if it wouldn't result in so much pleasure she might combust, but if this past week was any experience, Zoe was pretty sure they would both get off so many times they would lose count. Roslyn stood up and headed for the door, locking it this time.

Tossing a look over her shoulder, she moved into between Zoe and the desk, bending over and pulling her skirt up to reveal a black lace thong. Zoe's heart thundered, and she reached forward, unable to resist touching.

"Fuck me hard," Roslyn ordered, her command soft.

Standing to comply, Zoe ran her fingers over the curve of her ass in gentle patterns before she slapped her, the sound sharp. Roslyn grunted but smiled when she looked over her shoulder.

"Do it again."

Zoe spanked her several times before she slid three fingers inside her and began a brutal rhythm. The fear of being interrupted again didn't leave the back of her mind, only this time they wouldn't be able to hide it. While Roslyn might say she wouldn't fire her, that didn't mean the board wouldn't if they found out what the two of them were doing, in the office even.

Roslyn was soaking as Zoe plunged her fingers in and out. Eventually, when Roslyn was writhing enough, she bent down and used her mouth, pressing into Roslyn from behind and abandoning using her fingers. Roslyn gripped the far edge of the desk as she held on, Zoe pushing into her harder to give Roslyn as much friction as possible.

Her voice filled the room as she came, Zoe lapping up as

much as she could. She smoothed her hands over Roslyn's soft flesh and held her there for a minute before helping her to stand. She was straightening her skirt and fixing her hair when Roslyn captured her chin and raised her face to meet their mouths in a tender kiss.

"I always knew there was something different about you," Roslyn said, wiping the rest of her juices from Zoe's mouth. "I'm glad I finally found out what it was."

"Ms. Fudala–"

"I think you should call me Roslyn."

Zoe's heart thudded hard, and she repeated the name. "Roslyn." It felt so weird rolling off her tongue, but at the same time it felt good. Biting her lip, she stared into those light blue eyes as she desperately searched for an answer. "What are we doing?"

Roslyn's cheeks pulled tight as she smiled, a blush rising to her cheeks. She fixed her skirt and leaned against the desk, sitting like she had when she came out, but her blouse was still unbuttoned too far. Instinctively, Zoe reached forward to put them back into place. When she finished, Roslyn cupped her cheek. "What do you want to do? And before you say nothing, Zoe, I need an actual answer this time."

Zoe's lips parted in surprise at being called out, but she knew Roslyn was right. They had to come to some sort of resolution and boundaries.

"I'll state for the record that what we have right now I'm very comfortable with. I would love to continue it."

Nodding, Zoe ran gentle fingers over Roslyn's neck and collarbone before dropping her hands to her sides. "I've only ever fantasized about this."

Roslyn's lips twitched as she whispered, "Me too."

Zoe locked their gazes together, not quite believing what she heard. "I don't know what to say."

"Say you want me."

"I've always wanted you," Zoe murmured. "That's never been a question."

"Good." Roslyn moved in swiftly and brought their mouths together. "We'll figure out the rest as we go."

"Yeah," Zoe muttered, her mind going to mush as Roslyn stood up and kissed her again. "But if you want me to get actual work done, that is going to have to be limited."

Roslyn chuckled, her cheeks flushed with that after sex glow as she nodded and moved around the desk, toward her office, leaving Zoe on her own. She called over her shoulder as she shut the door, "If you think so, silly girl."

Collapsing into her desk chair, Zoe brushed her fingers over her face. "I'm so fucked."

ABOUT THE AUTHOR

Adrian J. Smith has been writing nearly her entire life but publishing since 2013. AJ jumps genres from action-packed police procedurals to the seedier life of vampires and witches to sweet romances with a May-December twist. She loves writing and reading about women in the midst of the ordinariness of life. AJ currently lives in Cheyenne, WY and plays the roles of author, wife, mother to two rambunctious kids, and occasional handy-woman.

- Website: https://adrianjsmithbooks.com/

- Facebook: https://www.facebook.com/adrianjsmithbooks

- Twitter: https://twitter.com/adrianajsmith

- Instagram: https://www.instagram.com/adrianjsmithbooks/

STRAWBERRY SQUASH

ELLE ARMSTRONG

The heat of the summer was nothing compared to the heat in her eyes. I watched as she casually bent over to pick more strawberries from the plants that were spaced out in neat rows. Row upon row upon row. Her cut-off jean shorts rose high up her buttocks when she leaned over, giving me a glorious view.

It was our job to empty the rows of their vibrant fruits and they had assigned me to a field with five pickers, including her. Her eyes smouldered every time our gazes met and I'm pretty sure mine seared into her, too. I had to look away for fear of wanting to rip her clothes off there and then, and take her among the plants. I could almost taste the tangy strawberry juice that would stick to her body as I made my way down to taste her cream.

"Who writes this rubbish?" Isla said with a deep sigh.

"Keep reading it. You'll enjoy the part where they turn themselves into strawberry jam!" Sandie replied and winked at her.

Isla wasn't so sure. She and Sandie had been best friends since high school. Sandie had 'developed early' as her mother put it, meaning she'd started her periods and grown a magnificent pair of breasts by the age of thirteen.

When they reached fifteen, Isla had an A cup bust and her first introduction to a woman's monthly torture. She was way behind Sandie in sexual experience too, only ever having had a handful of one-night-stands. For Sandie, this was her average weekend tally. How they stayed so close was anyone's guess. They were like chalk and cheese.

Sandie had talked Isla into picking strawberries on a farm in a village near York for the summer. York wasn't too far from home, but it was a stay in a field in a tent job, so it seemed like quite an adventure. Sandie had said that it was one last hurrah before they both settled into employment after finishing

University. Isla couldn't argue when Sandie applied logic to situations. Not that she did very often, but this one was definitely sound thinking.

They only had two days before they left, and Isla was frantically packing and unpacking as every time she finished, she realised she would never fit everything in her tent. Taking out all but the bare essentials, she started packing again, only adding any extra things back in that she deemed absolutely necessary. Unfortunately, when she'd finished, she kept finding she had nearly as much stuff as before.

Sandie had convinced Isla that it was sensible for them to do some preparation. Her grand idea was to spend hours watching online videos with any hints and tips on obtaining a good picking technique. She also encouraged Isla to read as many sapphic books as they could find that had the slightest possibility of strawberry picking being mentioned in them. Isla didn't think that would help in the slightest but she loved reading so went along with it.

Isla loved a good romance, with the prerequisite happy ending, whereas Sandie usually picked up erotica as her preferred genre. Isla's search was fruitless, until she found one book that featured their chosen holiday job, absurdly called 'Strawberry Girls get their Cream'.

The strange title had intrigued Isla. Upon opening it, she found the novel was more to Sandie's taste with lots of sex in the sun and not a care where the strawberry pips ended up. Isla learnt a few new things from reading the book, though. Next time she met someone, she would see if they would be open to some juicy roleplaying.

"You got your sunscreen on?" Sandie shouted to her from the strawberry row next to Isla's. It was their first day at the farm and on arrival, Isla had been happy to see that their accommodation came with not only an outside toilet as expected but also a large shower block.

They'd left their luggage in a small shed at the entrance to the field they'd be camping in, and after an extremely quick tour of the farm, they'd got straight to work.

They left anything they needed during the day at tables that were placed at the end of every fourth row, stocked with water.

"Yes mum," Isla said, but secretly she was relieved Sandie had mentioned it. Whilst every part of skin that the sun could kiss was slathered in factor fifty, she'd forgotten to put her baseball cap back on after picking up some water. Isla headed back to the table, thinking about where she might pitch her tent in the large field, when she collided with another picker who was sauntering past.

"Watch it!" the woman said. Her tone of voice was hard and unforgiving.

"I'm so sorry I didn't see you."

Black sunglasses covered the woman's eyes, and a baseball cap left her upper face in shadow, but Isla was sure she was glaring at her. There was a tense silence as they sized each other up.

"Yeah, well, just watch where you're going!" With that, the woman continued, swaggering her way past Isla wearing an eye-catching brown, short-sleeved T-shirt and khaki shorts that only just covered her modesty. Isla felt like she'd met her before. Her voice rang little bells in the back of her mind, but Isla would never spend time with someone so rude. Although with legs like hers, she could be persuaded.

Isla quickly grabbed her cap from the refreshment table and placed it on her head, carefully pulling her ponytail through the hole at the back. As she turned to go back to the start of the fruit in her row, she saw the woman saunter down another row three along from hers. There was something entrancing about her; a pull that Isla was struggling to fight against.

As if sensing she was being watched, the woman turned and looked towards Isla. Instead of being a romantic moment between them, with little hearts bubbling up from the top of their heads and longing looks, the woman put her hands on her hips with her feet aggressively apart. Isla gulped and sprinted back to where she had left her half-filled basket. There was no way she'd be getting her jam on with her.

Soon she was back in the groove of pick, throw in basket, pick, throw, repeat a zillion times. Every so often, Isla couldn't resist shooting a quick glance over her shoulder, each time finding the woman with her head turned in her direction.

The sharp blast of the end of the day hooter rang across the fields, making Isla jump and causing her stomach to meet her tonsils. She rubbed her back, straightened her arms in the air, and stretched. She ached all over and was certain she'd discovered previously unknown muscles. Sandie had disappeared somewhere ahead of her, but Isla took her time trying to stretch some of the aches away as she walked. What she really wanted to do would be to soak in a hot bath and relax with a glass of wine.

Reality smacked her in the face as the heat caused a drop of sweat to fall onto her nose from her forehead. Taking in her surroundings, she realised a quick shower in the shower block, where no doubt the warm water would have already run out before she got there, was more likely in her future. A cold shower didn't seem so bad though, considering the heat of the day was making her feel like every drop of blood in her body had reached boiling point.

She searched for Sandie, and after several minutes, found her standing far too near to be friendly by a gorgeous redhead. Walking over, Isla coughed loudly to announce her arrival. Sandie startled, then grinned when she saw her.

"I thought I'd grab a shower, then take some food back to my tent tonight. I'm shattered," Isla said. A quick look of relief swept over Sandie's face before she schooled her expression into one of fake disappointment.

"Are you sure? This is Francis. We were just going to organise meeting up for dinner tonight."

"I'm sure. The top of the field is going to be a lot quieter, so I'm going to pitch my tent up there. I'm worn out. I'm not used to doing manual labour after sitting in a classroom for years. Plus, I really need some downtime. Is that okay?"

"Yes, of course. I mean, I thought I'd pitch mine somewhere here." Sandie pointed in a vague direction towards an area close by, where another tent was already half pitched, well away from the others. It didn't need Einstein to figure out which friendly redhead it belonged to.

"Of course. I'll probably read for a little while, then sleep for hours."

"Any problems, you come and get me, okay?"

Isla nodded, knowing full well that neither of them wanted that to happen. "Right, I'm off. I need to get my tent unpacked and put up, then shower." Isla waved over her shoulder as she hastily walked away. Her tent was only a small two person one, and she'd have it up in no time. She longed for solitude, knowing it was highly unlikely she would find her own 'Francis', and she had no desire to listen to any of the other people who were hooking up around her. At least up the small rise at the top end, there was only one other solitary tent pitched.

Isla made quick work of putting up her tent. She left a respectable distance between herself and her neighbour, so they could each have their privacy.

After she'd showered and changed, she grabbed some food from the dining area, which was really just a barn that had been converted and took it back to her tent. Isla was glad she'd had the foresight to put her pyjamas on under her clothes after showering, so all she had to do was tidy away her rubbish in a sealable bag and remove her outer clothes.

She'd just crawled into her sleeping bag when she heard footsteps approaching. Deciding it must be her neighbour, Isla was extremely tempted to unzip her tent so she could peek out to see who it was. The sound of her zipper being pulled up forcibly took that decision away from her.

"What the bloody hell do you think you're doing, pitching back here?"

The venom and anger in the voice made Isla shrink back as far as the frame of her tent would allow. It was definitely a female, and she sounded familiar, which couldn't be right, as Isla had been too shy to make any friends on her first day. She had Sandie for that, anyway.

Isla quickly covered her eyes with her arm as a blinding light burned into her retinas and illuminated her tent.

"Oh, for fuck's sake. If it isn't 'Little Miss Uppity Bitch'," the torch holder sneered.

Isla was at a disadvantage as the blinding torch beam meant she couldn't see who the person invading her tent was. The beam was so bright it was like being in front of a spotlight. Isla kept her arm firmly over her eyes.

"I, er, well, I thought it was an open field. That you could pitch anywhere in it."

"I *thought it was an open field, blah blah,*" the voice taunted in a very poor imitation of her own.

"Who are you? You sound kind of familiar, but not. And that was a crap impersonation of me!"

"Are you even for real?" the woman asked, with what sounded like disbelief. But why would she take that tone with Isla?

Isla was tired and achy after her first day of manual work, and felt the last of her manners roll onto the floor and away down the field.

"Look," she said sharply. "I really don't know who you are or who you think you are, but could you please get out of my tent so I can get some sleep?"

Silence. Strange? It seemed to have gone dark suddenly too. She'd been sure there'd be some sort of counterattack. Slowly lowering her arm, Isla realised she was on her own. Only the swaying of the tent flaps was evidence that someone had actually been there at all.

"Crock-a-rudel-rooooo!"

Isla startled awake at the piercing sound. Weren't roosters meant to say cock-a-doodle-do? Maybe this one was from overseas and had a slight accent? After rubbing her eyes, Isla blearily tried to focus on her watch. Five in the morning. Wait, what? Five as in A.M? What the blazes?

Snuggling herself into a tight cocoon within her sleeping bag, Isla tried to blot out the sounds of the wildlife and get back to sleep.

The nearby sound of a tent zip opening awoke her a second time. Isla scrambled in her bag, desperately trying to escape its clutches so she could properly see who her rude neighbour was.

By the time she'd freed herself and opened her own tent zip, all she could see was the back of the woman walking down towards the food barn. Isla made a mental note of what the woman was wearing, determined to identify her later. Something was knocking on the door of her memory, wanting to be let in so it could tell her a secret.

Dark hair in a ponytail that was sticking through the gap at the back of a cap was swinging from side to side as she walked. Denim shorts that were just that—short! Phew, was it getting warm suddenly? A navy-blue vest top completed the outfit. Nope, Isla was still none the wiser, but the temperature had definitely risen in the tent.

Now she'd seen the outfit the girl was wearing; she was on a mission to hunt her down. One thing she was certain of was that the woman from the tent was the same one she'd ploughed into yesterday. After tossing and turning for some considerable time the night before, Isla had realised they both had the same petulant voice.

The sun kept disappearing behind fluffy white clouds, making the heat a little more bearable. Isla straightened and pushed one fist into her back to straighten out the kinks, whilst the other mopped her brow. She'd found a groove now, which helped minimise the number of muscles being stretched. Now she was being more efficient, the number of baskets she'd filled was nearly double than the day before, and the working day still wasn't over.

Isla had kept an eye out all day for her neighbour but hadn't found her. The farm's owners had split them into two groups and sent one over to another field. Isla surmised the girl must be in that group, along with Francis, much to Sandie's dismay. It was bizarre, but she reminded Isla of one of her one-night-stands. She'd been lovely and gentle, and not in the least bit confrontational. So, it definitely wasn't her!

Isla would always regret that the only thing they'd bothered swapping that night was bodily fluids, instead of adding names and phone numbers into the mix.

As soon as the clock was up for the day, Sandie grabbed Isla's hand and made a beeline for the other field. She tugged Isla cave-woman style behind her, but Isla was okay with that, as her curiosity grew, to see if her elusive neighbour was amongst the workers in the distance. When they reached the field, they were packing up their gloves and baskets.

Standing to the side as everyone began walking out of the field, Isla felt like a sentry keeping watch, checking everyone's clothing, then faces.

"Ooh, here comes Francis!" Sandie shouted, making Isla jump. She'd been too busy looking at some very nice bare legs to notice who was approaching.

"She's got her friend with her. Let's go say hi."

Isla glanced up and noticed the very vibrant red-haired Francis walking towards them. Isla thought she might be with someone wearing a cap, but they blended into the group of workers exiting the field, and she couldn't tell for sure.

She quickly lowered her gaze to find the shorts that were

seared into her memory. She was desperate to confirm who this neighbour of hers was.

"Come on," Francis said, loud enough to hear. "Come and meet my new friends."

Finally, Isla spotted a pair of tanned legs with obscenely short shorts walking towards her. Working her way up, she identified the blue vest top as the one she'd seen that morning, which left the person's fa — Oh no, it couldn't be!

Francis pulled at her friend, as Sandie tugged Isla and they walked towards each other like opposing armies. Sandie and Francis completely spoiled the image by smiling brightly at each other.

"Hi..." Sandie said, holding her hand out to the scowling tent invader.

Francis, none too gently nudged her friend. The girl took off her sunglasses and Isla's world spun upside down, inside out, and left her insides all wobbly like they were made of goop.

"Freya," grunted the torch wielding maniac. A quick handshake, so quick that if you blinked, you'd miss it. Sandie, bless her, didn't seem to know what to make of her new plaything's friend. Nor did she come to think of it.

Isla frowned as she played the name on a loop through her head. Freyah, Freya-ya, Freyaaaaa. Nope, no matter how she pronounced it, the name did not fit the seething ball of anger standing in front of her.

Everyone's eyes turned to her and Isla hadn't a clue what she'd done wrong. An expectant silence made her want to start backing away slowly. Isla turned to Sandie and furrowed her brows.

"Gah!" Sandie heaved a sigh of frustration. "This is Isla."

Oh, OH! Formalities. She was supposed to be introducing herself. It was good manners apparently.

There again, Freya didn't deserve any form of social

etiquette after her rudeness the night before. But it was good to be the better person, so Isla stuck her hand out forcefully towards the woman.

Freya, however, had obviously failed etiquette school as she stood glaring at Isla's hand. "How ya doing, Freyaaaaaa?"

Isla knew she was dicing with death when the dark brown eyes, fixed on her, turned murderous. Freya's hands balled into tight fists as she took a menacing step closer to Isla.

Isla swallowed. She'd never been in the path of a tornado before; but the way Freya was looking at her gave her certain knowledge that she was going to be chewed up, messed with, then spat back out again. There were parts of her life that even Sandie didn't know about, and whilst the Tornado was angry at her, she knew it wasn't entirely because of the tent.

Freya took another step closer and seemed to double in size as she towered above Isla. "Move. Your. Tent!"

Or maybe it was? Francis obviously decided now was a good time to intervene as she made a grab for her friend and started dragging her out of the field. "See you at dinner," Francis called over her shoulder, as she pulled Freya along with her.

"What's her problem?" Sandie whispered as she grabbed hold of Isla and yanked her in the same direction.

"I put my tent up near hers. It would seem she objects to having neighbours. Hard to understand when she's obviously such a social butterfly."

"Behave, I really like Francis. Like, *really* like her."

"You've only known her for just over a day. How can you tell it's not just lust?" Isla stopped their progression and turned to look at her friend's face. She nearly fell over with shock when she saw the little hearts in her best friend's eyes where her pupils used to be.

Shit.

It was an awkward dinner, with Isla setting a new world record for uncomfortably looking at a wristwatch in one hour.

She almost ran out of the dining barn when she'd finished her meal, eager to put as much distance as she could between herself and Freya. If looks could kill, Isla knew she'd have been on the floor maybe forty times. Perhaps that was a new world record too? Luckily for her, the other three were still drinking coffees and making a dismal attempt at small talk.

Grabbing her wash bag and towel, Isla raced to the showers, hoping she could finish and get back to her tent before Freya left the dining room. Isla had eaten far too many delicious, soft, juicy strawberries to leave room to stomach any more aggravation.

Everything was quiet as she walked back up the slight incline to her tent. Isla's heart rate slowed as she pulled the zipper up in her tent and clambered inside.

She'd just made herself comfy using her sleeping bag to pad the ground a bit when a sharp blast of music assaulted her ears. Drum and cymbals quickly joined a guitar riff, which was closely followed by a loud screech melding eventually into the voice of the singer. She really wasn't sure that word was the best descriptor, as it sounded more like a wolf in pain.

Isla quickly shuffled her bum to the tent opening and undid the zip, causing it to make a sound eerily similar to the night before. In just her pyjamas and flip-flops, she strode over to Freya's tent.

"Hey Freya!" Isla tried to shout above the din pounding from inside the tent. Quickly realising it was a lost cause, she re-enacted the night before. Grabbing the zipper, she yanked the entrance to her neighbour's tent open. It was just before dusk, but there was still enough light to stop Isla firmly in her tracks when she caught sight of the infuriating woman.

Freya's tent was a lot larger than her own and had more room for belongings. There, sitting casually on a camping chair, one leg crossed over the other, sat Freya. A very nude, not got a stitch of clothing on, Freya.

Isla's eyes opened wide and she was suddenly back in her bedroom three years ago. A juddering breath catapulted her back to the present. Fear of being yelled at mixed with excitement as she couldn't help but admire the hard, yet somehow still soft, plains of her neighbour's body. Freya tapped her phone and suddenly the music stopped as abruptly as it had started.

"You gonna stand there all day, or are you coming in?" Freya asked, as she eyed Isla from the top of her head down to her pyjamas.

Isla, who was standing frozen at the flap of the tent, suddenly sparked to life. She hastily pulled the tent zip back down, then walked up to Freya and stood before her with her hands on her hips.

"So, you wanted my attention? You got it!"

Freya stood up and Isla had to use all her self-control to stop herself from reaching out to take one of a pair of delectable breasts in her hand.

"Are you going to take off those pyjamas, or do you want me to do it for you?"

"What makes you so sure I want you?" Isla bucked her head to the side as she studied Freya's face. Well, that and a couple of things further south.

"You want me all right! You might try to act like Little Miss Uppity Bitch, but your eyes give you away." Freya's voice was cocky and her own eyes held a challenge.

"Right yeah, my eyes. The ones that narrow every time I

see you. What the hell have you been doing, anyway? You're calling me a bitch, but have you looked in the mirror lately?"

A silent standoff followed, as they both glared at each other. The tension fuelled the fire simmering in Isla. Thinking no further, Isla reached out and grabbed Freya by the back of her neck, pulling her into a bruising, full on tongues the lot kiss.

Only when Isla felt like her lungs would collapse in on themselves from being empty did she break the kiss and gulp in some much needed air.

"Let's get one thing clear from the start. Tonight, I am in charge here! You will do what I say, when I say, and how I say. Am I making myself clear?" Isla injected as much authority into her voice as she could muster.

"Crystal clear." Freya spoke the words, but her eyes locked onto Isla's defiantly.

"Keep talking like that and I'll have no choice but to take off my flip-flop!" Isla warned as she scowled back at Freya.

"Is that a promise or a threat?"

"Both!" Isla shrugged off her pyjama top, then threw the shorts down and kicked them off when they reached her feet.

Her flip-flops inadvertently flew off too, flying into the side of the tent and pushing the material outwards, and causing it to ripple. No worries, she could still reach them in the confinements of the tent.

"Have you got anything with you I can use to tie your hands together?" Isla asked as a warm heat settled all over her. She watched as Freya's eyes lazily ran over her body before coming up to meet her own. Isla gasped when she saw the want, the desire shining in them.

"Yeah, I've got a belt on my jeans. Hang on." Freya leant over towards her case, that was shoved in a corner to her left side. The tent, whilst bigger than Isla's, was still compact, with most things within an arm's reach.

"Great, I'm going to fetch my sleeping bag so we can make ourselves more comfortable."

"Like that? You've got no clothes on." Freya looked back up. Her mouth widened into an O, causing a very unladylike snort to escape Isla's mouth.

Isla quickly exited the tent in all her nude glory and retrieved her sleeping bag and her few valuables, namely her phone and her bumbag.

She let herself back into Freya's tent and handed her the sleeping bag in exchange for the belt. It was a leather belt, still quite unyielding, but she'd make it work. Isla bent and manipulated it a few times to loosen some of the tension. Freya meanwhile had created a cosy little nest for them to lie on.

Freya straightened and wrapped her arms around Isla. Isla immediately searched for her lips when Freya bent her head towards her. Pulling back sharply, she urged Freya's arms forward and tied the belt around her wrists as best she could. It was a little loose, but hopefully would still do the job of reminding Freya to keep her hands to herself. Despite Freya being a lot taller and more muscular than her, Isla manhandled her down onto the makeshift bed.

"Tell me what you want and I'll do my best to deliver," Isla said as she lowered herself down onto the sleeping bags beside Freya and tugged Freya's bound arms above her head, allowing the elbows to bend so it was more comfortable. Isla knew she would never become a Domme like the Strawberry picking woman in the erotica book that Sandie had found. She was too soft, but it was fun trying.

"What... what you said, you know? With the flip-flop." Freya's voice had lost all trace of stubbornness. Longing was replacing it instead, causing a shiver to run through Isla and goosebumps to rise along her arms in answering lust.

"Kiss me!" Isla put every ounce of self-control she had left into her voice, but she was desperately losing the battle to remain in control of Freya and, more importantly, herself.

Freya half sat, and Isla leaned in so their lips could meet in a fiery kiss that stoked the embers until they were blazing again. Isla slowly lowered them back into a horizontal position and lay fully on top of Freya, pinning her to the bedding.

Unhurriedly, she let her hand wander, easing herself off Freya slightly to allow her to find one of the delicious breasts she had dreamt about on more than one occasion in the last three years. Circling the nub that was hardening with every tiny circuit, Isla waited till it was just right before squeezing it tightly between her thumb and forefinger. Then there was rubbing, pinching, stroking, grabbing, as Isla's hand kept up a steady onslaught.

Freya groaned into her mouth as their kiss became harder, tongues demanding to become entwined, lips being gently bitten and pulled between teeth as mouths disconnected with a pop, only to meet up again in a kiss even more frantic, more bruising, more everything. All the pent-up passion ignited, the heat stroking Isla's back as if trying to replace where her lover's hands should be.

Finishing with one breast, Isla swapped to the other, and lavished it with the same attention, twisting, nipping, tickling, rolling. Isla kissed from one shoulder blade to the other as her hand worked Freya's nipple into a tight, firm bud. Once she'd had her fill, Isla's hand began working its way down Freya's body, finding then running her fingers through wet heat as she sought her entrance.

Without preamble, Isla entered Freya with three fingers. One, two, three thrusts and Freya's walls were tightening around her. Four, five, and she was coming, her walls pulsating a hypnotising rhythm as Isla swiftly moved her fingers back and forth to the tempo being created. Freya came again with a soft cry when Isla used her thumb to flick her clit.

Easing up on her, Isla slowly withdrew her fingers and held Freya as she smouldered through the aftershocks. When Freya's trembling body stilled, Isla delivered another hard kiss to succulent lips she wanted to kiss forever. Freya was kissing her back with matching intensity and together they worked up a sweat as they kissed away the frustration, the years, and the missed opportunities since they'd last seen each other.

Reluctantly, Isla slowly withdrew from Freya's warm, welcoming body. Her arm reached out and scrambled around, searching for, ah, there it was.

"Turn over," Isla commanded. "On your knees, arms in front."

Eagerly, Freya rolled over and with help from Isla to steady her, she assumed the position, her body trembling slightly with what Isla assumed was excitement and arousal. Both were coursing through her body as she admired the view in front of her. Unable to help herself, she caressed the bottom that was so tantalising.

"Ohhhh," Freya's sigh sent a voltage of electricity straight through Isla as a new bolt of arousal took her dangerously close to the edge.

Withdrawing her hand, Isla took the item she'd found and wiped it along the bedding to make sure it was clean. The flip-flops were new, so they were already relatively clean.

"Are your wrists okay with the belt still? You're not uncomfortable like that?" To be fair, Freya didn't look uncomfortable. On her knees, she looked like she was praying with her hands held together in front of her, resting on the sleeping bags.

"Nah, I'm good."

"Do you have a safe word, just in case?" Isla asked.

"Strawberry Squash."

Isla chuckled. Here was the woman she had far too briefly encountered before. No wonder she hadn't recognised her? This Freya was witty and warm; so very different from the Incredible Sulk she'd encountered at the farm so far.

"Strawberry Squash it is then. Am I okay to use my flip-flop on your delectable arse?"

"Please," came the half-strangled reply.

Isla again ran her hand over the smooth, lush, bum cheek before *thwack*! The first blow she delivered was firm, but not too hard.

"Arghhh," Freya flinched as the flip-flop connected with her. Isla checked in with her to make sure she was okay, then delivered a teasing caress with her hand that drifted between her legs and stroked her clit softly.

Slowly pulling her hand back, Isla waited a beat, then another. The next blow with the flip-flop was heavier, making a loud smacking noise as it connected with skin.

"Oh, oh, ahhh, do it again!" Freya begged as her breathing grew laboured.

Not wanting it to be over too soon, the next two hits were softer, with gentle caresses by her hands in between. Isla ghosted her hand over Freya's entrance, pleased to find her excitement was overflowing, coating her folds, and mingling with the juices her earlier orgasms had created.

"Isle's please!"

Isle's? I quite like that. Isla took the hint and delivered five hard hits to one butt cheek, followed by another five hard hits to the other. Freya's bottom glowed red in the muted light cast from the camping lantern in the tent's corner.

Draping herself halfway over Freya's back, Isla shifted her position till she could reach between Freya's legs from behind. Slowly running her fingers through pooling wetness, Isla's fingers sailed along smoothly until they reached the hard nub at the apex of Freya's legs.

Using her other hand, she ran it down the front, swapping with the first hand and taking over the care of the precious bundle of nerves. The freed hand leisurely inched its way back to the puckered skin at the back of the valley. Lightly putting pressure there, her hands worked in tandem, mirroring their movements. Applying further pressure to both, Isla pinched at Freya's clit, whilst still rubbing her from behind.

"Oh, bloody hell Isla, oh goodness, yes, oh yes."

Isla smirked as she increased her efforts, knowing it wouldn't be long now until Freya exploded. Although the angle was straining the muscles in her arms, she wouldn't, couldn't, stop now.

"Fuck, oh fuck, oh fuck, ahhhhhhh!" Freya climaxed and if the wetness filling Isla's hand was any indication, she'd come hard.

Isla slipped off Freya's back and lay down on the bedding. Freya collapsed next to her, and Isla quickly undid the belt to free her hands. Reaching for Freya, she pulled her in close and somehow wrapped the taller woman into a tight cocoon. They stayed that way for several minutes, both steadying their erratic breathing.

Like a butterfly awakening from its chrysalis, Freya peeled herself away from Isla with a wide grin on her face. Isla's heart beat double time as she stared in wonder at how beautiful she really was, her transformation from angry caterpillar complete.

"What?" Freya asked with a confused expression.

"Sorry, I was just admiring how beautiful you are."

"Right back at cha. Please, will you roll over? I'd like to take my turn."

"Well, it would be rude not to, I suppose." Isla winked as she rolled onto her back.

Freya's tongue was everywhere at once, sucking, flicking, then licking her clit. The momentum was building closer with every nibble, every slow then quick suck until finally Isla was seeing fireworks. That was all she could see. Sparks were bouncing off her eyelids as she threw her head back, eyes closed. Her knees gripped Freya's head below as she rocketed along to the most spectacular orgasm she'd ever had. It was even better than the previous three climaxes this wicked tongue had delivered.

Freya didn't let up on her and sucked Isla fully into her mouth, creating more aftershocks before releasing her and once more tongue fucking her, with the occasional flick of the clit, into oblivion.

"Ah Freya, stop, I can't, I can't." But she could as a nip at her clit and a wicked tongue sent her back into the stratosphere once again.

Legs weak and trembling, Isla threw herself to the right of Freya and took a deep breath. "Wow!"

"You're amazing Isle's. Let me know when you're ready to go again."

"No way. Give me a minute, then I think it's time I tasted you."

"Ready when you are!"

Isla turned over and found Freya splayed over the sleeping bags. The tents were too small to spread out fully and Isla was already half lying on top of Freya. Isla shifted herself down until she was staring right into Freya's glistening entrance. Grabbing one leg, Isla mustered up strength from the hidden reserves buried within her and threw it over her shoulder. The other leg followed suit, over the other shoulder, as the flames she could feel flickering inside roared and flared through her body.

"Keep still. Do not move until I can say you can move. Do not come till I say you can come. Comprendy?"

"Yes, please, now, yes."

Isla lowered her head, with the sole intention of driving Freya into a lust filled frenzy, before giving her the most earth-shattering orgasm she was capable of. It was going to be a long night!

The next morning, Isla was sure she was doing a good impersonation of a duck as she rushed down the hill towards the fields. Checking the assignment sheet, it dismayed her to see she was in the row next to Sandie. She was bound to notice the tired and stiff way she was moving around. Isla wasn't ready to face the grilling her best friend would, without a doubt, deliver. She was further disheartened to see that Freya and Francis weren't working in the same field as them. There would be no secret glances and admiring looks today.

Isla's muscles strained and protested when she started picking the juicy strawberries. The sweet, fruity smell made her stomach rumble, and she slipped a couple into her mouth surreptitiously, having missed breakfast. She'd left Freya's tent mere minutes ago, frantically changing into her work clothes before dashing to make it and start picking on time.

They'd fallen asleep in the early hours, sated and exhausted, and had missed the first alarm call from Rodney, the farm's resident rooster. Isla had soon learnt his name yesterday, after listening to her fellow pickers swearing and ranting about all the things they would do to the rooster and all the ways they could cook and garnish him.

The snooze button got hit around ten times following the first phone alarm, making them very late when they wearily climbed out of the sleeping bag.

They'd zipped the ends of their sleeping bags together in a way that formed a double sleeping bag. A warm, cosy, toasty, double bag.

"Okay spill. Why are you walking like you've shit yourself?!"

The grilling from Sandie started as soon as the hooter went to signal the working day was over. It was still being conducted as they ate their evening meal in the barn. Finally, at seven twenty, when Francis and Freya joined their table, the grilling became a roasting as Sandie and Francis joined the dots, and demanded to know every single detail.

Isla's cheeks were on fire as she gave them a very watered-down version of the night before. Freya looked quite bemused as she watched Isla being bombarded with question after question.

Finally, it ended when Francis and Sandie decided there were much better things to be doing than tormenting their friends. Isla set off back up the hill and jumped when a hand reached out and took her own. They walked lazily back to their tents with their hands swinging between them and a catcall or two from the now very recently relegated to former best friends who, of course, turned their way and noticed their public display of affection.

"I need a shower," Isla stated as she stood in the gap separating their two tents.

"Sounds good to me. Mind if I join you?"

Isla shot her a look that left no room for misinterpretation, and disappeared back to her tent to get her shower things, rejoining Freya a couple of minutes later. Isla couldn't believe there was no one in the shower block when they arrived. Not one to pass up an opportunity, Isla pulled Freya into one of the shower stalls as soon as they were both undressed. Turning the shower on, the lukewarm water provided a clue why they were alone. Isla didn't care. As long as it remained warm to tepid, it would suffice.

Pushing Freya up against the shower wall, Isla kissed her hungrily, making up for the hours they had worked separately. *Oh god I have it bad!*

Freya wrapped her arms around Isla's neck and returned the kiss like she, too, was starving. Without breaking the kiss, Freya ushered them under the showerhead and let the still warm water sluice all over them. They were soaking wet in seconds.

Isla pushed back and once she had Freya pinned against the wall, she massaged her breasts as she lowered herself to Freya's dark curls. Reluctantly leaving the enticing pair, she used one hand to part Freya's folds. Using the other hand, she teased Freya's clit with little flicks.

Freya was backed up flush against the wall with her hands braced by her sides, flat against it. Isla looked up into Freya's gorgeous brown eyes. On receiving the nod, she ran her hand along the edge of Freya's entrance before entering her with two fingers. Gently, she probed until she found her sensitive spot. Curling her fingers, she rubbed softly against her G-spot, whilst her other hand drifted through her folds until they lazily found Freya's already pulsating clit.

Once there, Isla wasted no time and squeezed Freya's clit between her forefinger and thumb as her other fingers caressed the textured area inside that she knew would deliver pleasure instantly. Squeezing and rubbing, she worked her hands as Freya trembled, getting closer to the edge remarkably quickly.

Trying her best to support Freya, who was gradually sliding down the shower wall, Isla gave her clit a firm pinch as she continued to stroke her sensitive spot.

"Ahhhh, urghhhffff." Isla looked up in time to witness Freya's mouth go from shouting her ecstasy, to being filled with shower water, causing her to cough violently.

"Pffffrrrr, jeez," cough, "bloody hell," cough.

Isla quickly removed her hands and supported Freya by holding her under her armpits until Freya gradually took back control of her body. Isla withdrew her hands and used them to pull Freya's face lower and into a soft kiss.

Freya broke it first. "Bloody hell, Isle, that was intense. And I don't mean my near drowning at the end. Let's get clean, then I'll return the favour when we're on dry land."

"Aye, aye Captain. Pass me the soap."

Freya made good on her promise and Isla had never felt so fulfilled and happy as she did, laying in her arms quite some time later.

"Freya, can I ask you something?" Not waiting for a response, Isla took a deep breath. "Why were you being so horrid those first few days?" Isla purposely kept her tone soft.

"You're joking, right? You were ignoring me the whole time!"

Isla winced at the hurt in Freya's voice. "I only realised it was you when we came to meet Francis yesterday afternoon." She sat up so she could face Freya.

The look Freya shot her said she clearly didn't believe her. "The first time we met, you had a cap and sunglasses hiding most of your face. I thought you seemed familiar, but you were so mean. Why were you?" Now it was Isla's tone that was laced with hurt.

"I didn't realise when we collided, but then when I saw it was you, I expected you to talk to me and say hi. But you treated me like a complete stranger. That hurt Isla. I know the timing sucked the last time we met, with you going away to university just a couple of days after. But I thought if, or should that be when, we saw each other again, that we'd be able to, I don't know... reconnect, I suppose."

"Oh Freya, I'm so sorry. I honestly didn't recognise you. Three years is a long time for me to remember anything other than you naked underneath me. Then when you came into my tent, the torchlight blinded me and I couldn't see anything, let alone see that it was you."

"So?" Freya's voice somehow trembled on that one small word.

"So? I don't know what that means." Isla returned, praying the conversation wasn't about to turn into an argument.

"So, now you've finished university, where do we go from here?"

Isla reached out and took Freya's hand. All the colour had drained out of her face and her expression was so serious it caused a sharp pang in Isla's chest.

"Well, first, we move my tent over here, so we can store as much stuff in it as we can. That way, we'll have more room in here for us. Yes, that's right, I'm moving in. Any objections? No? Good. Then when we go home, we can go on dates and spend lots of time together and see how it goes. Then, if it's all still as good as it is now, we can build our future together. How does that sound?"

"That sounds perfect. I don't want the odd night here and there with you. I know now, more than ever, that I want you in my life. The connection we had that first time was surreal. Saying goodbye after our one night together just about did me in. I mean, we didn't even get each other's names. It was full on lust at first sight." Freya's tone told Isla she was being completely serious.

Isla chuckled and was relieved when Freya joined in. "As soon as you came and danced with me that night in the bar, I felt something. It was like my whole body woke up for the first time. Leaving with you soon after seemed as natural as breathing. Every part of me was in tune with you. Our bodies created a symphony when we finally touched skin to skin."

Isla paused as the night in question crashed into her memories in full force. "We got hot and heavy pretty quickly, didn't we? We didn't stop to find the time for pleasantries or names, like you said, or other inconsequential things."

Isla felt herself reacting just as her body had then, and a warm heat settled between her legs. "I only wish you hadn't had to leave at silly o'clock to go to work. Or that I'd been awake enough to get your details."

"Things happen the way they're meant to, even if it was the best night of my life, until last night anyway." Freya said as she lowered her lips to take Isla's. The kiss that followed was slow and sweet, causing goosebumps to erupt all along Isla's arms. She wrapped them around Freya's neck as she deepened the kiss and demanded her tongue be allowed entry to her lover's mouth. Jeez, this woman could kiss.

With their lips still locked, Freya lowered Isla down onto her back and lay down on top of her. Their breasts and thighs came together deliciously as their bodies blended together. Isla's last sensible thought was to wonder if they'd get caught if they were to have a midnight tryst in the strawberry rows.

ABOUT THE AUTHOR

Elle is from the north of the UK, meaning she automatically has an accent no one can understand. Deaf as a post and about as mobile as one, Elle fell into writing to pass the boredom of daytime TV. Her first book, A Marine's Conflict, was co-written with Jax Meyer and now Elle is going it alone with no clue what she's doing. Her motto right now is fake it till you make it.

- Website: https://ellearmstrong.com/

- Facebook: https://www.facebook.com/elle.armstrong.5876

- Twitter: https://twitter.com/ElleArmstrong19

THREE-HOUR DELAY

LL SHELTON

Gentle kisses mixed with soft nibbles sprinkled over the crook of my neck, leaving a trail of peppered goosebumps. My mouth lays agape with my back arching as I am hers for taking. Uncontrollable low moans get smothered by the darkness. My body is a raging forest fire, and this sexy woman is the match. Her fingers twist and pull gently at my nipple as they bloom like spring flowers. She controls all of me like an orchestra conductor, and my body is a symphony of lust. Her mouth travels, and when those lips engulf my stiff nipple, heat ascends into my cheeks, and electricity shoots between my legs straight into my clit. Her body covers me, all of me. Our hips mold perfectly with our bare mounds connecting with need. The motion of her ass grinds slowly and precisely, and we are in tune. Each rub and thrust drove me to a peak, an edge, and the point of no return. Her lips slip from my nipple as she holds my hands over my head. Her mouth takes to mine, and she kisses me like she needs oxygen to breathe. Nipple to nipple, clit to clit, our bodies become the pieces of a puzzle clued by small pebbles of sweat. Everything builds, slow, then faster, until there is no stopping our desires from becoming wants, then our wants evolve into needs. Every wall of mine crumbles into rubble. Hitches of breaths, moans and two bodies match in an ocean of explosion as we surge forward into a never-ending climax as one.

Tasha jumped when her phone rang. Her thoughts got lost in the memories of hours earlier with Erica, a gorgeous blonde she brought home from the local bar. One-night hookups weren't something Tasha made a habit of, but Erica was deliciously irresistible last night. The mere replay of their sex caused wetness to fill her panties. She glanced at the phone quickly to see her best friend's picture pop up. A roll of the eyes before she hits the answer button. Glass in hand, she takes a long sip of the rosy wine swirling in the long stemware.

The wine slipped into her throat before warming her insides. "Hello, Sandy."

"Whatcha doing?" The woman says on the other end.

The way Sandy dragged the words out tells Tasha she was digging for information. Sandy, married to the same man for fifteen years with the white picket fence, the three kids, and the yellow Labrador, lives vicariously through Tasha's single gay life.

Sandy continued in a whisper when Tasha didn't answer. "Is she still there?"

"No, she left. She had a redeye flight leaving this evening, so you can stop whispering."

"So, tell me. How was the pilot? Did she make you soar?"

"Ha! I'm not kissing and telling." Tasha leaned back while inhaling the sweetness of the wine. An evil smirk crossed her face; she wasn't sure if her and Erica's interlocked bodies or the enjoyment of teasing Sandy caused the grin. Truth be told, Erica made her more than soar.

"So, there is something to tell?" Sandy says.

"Oh god, Sandy. It was the best sex I've ever had; the woman was out of this world." Tasha stopped talking for a moment and listened. A second tap at the front door came. "Crap, now what?"

"What's the matter?"

"Um, hold on, Sandy. Let me call you back; someone is knocking on my door."

"You want me to hold on while you find out who it is? There was a robbery a few miles from you a couple of weeks ago. You can never be too safe. I can tell John to come over in his police car?"

"Sandy. Calm down. It's most likely just another Uber Eats driver at the wrong apartment. I'll be fine. Pay attention to that hot cop husband of yours. Call you later, buddy."

"You're not getting out of telling me the details with the pilot." Sandy's voice screamed from the phone as Tasha tapped the end button.

Adjusting the sash on her silk robe tighter, Tasha stopped to look in the mirror. Yep, she looked freshly fucked. The thought brought a smile that reached from ear to ear. Coming up on her tiptoes, she stretched her five-foot frame to its full length, peeked out of the peephole, and then fell back down to her heels. "What?" Not believing her eyes, Tasha took one more look before she unlocked the door and pulled it open.

"I thought," she says before the brightest smile stops her words. The woman, who left a few hours ago and whose smell still lingered on her sheets, stood in front of her.

"My plane got delayed by three hours. Most pilots headed to the airport's lounge." She stopped her words and leaned against the door frame. Her hand rested inside the pocket of her trousers. "I thought maybe you could help me pass my downtime."

Tasha swallowed hard. The taste of Erica lingered on her lips like the after sting of a shot of whiskey, so the sight of her standing there in a pilot's uniform with one leg crossed over the other got Tasha's juices flowing.

"What can I do to help with this downtime?"

"You can start by removing that robe."

Tasha's eyes never left the deep blue ones that stared back at her. She could feel the raw hunger growing in her depths. Her fingers dragged the sash with the material parting, revealing the mounds of her breast. Erica stood there biting her lower lip, and Tasha shifted to adjust to the throbbing between her legs. Her shoulders slipped out, and Tasha's hands grasped her breasts, keeping them hidden with a smidge of silk. Erica stepped toward her. She stepped back. The door closed, and the robe dropped to the floor.

"Beautiful," Erica whispered. "Come here."

Tasha took a step.

"Closer," Erica asked.

Another step and the heat between them became undeniable. Tasha's eyes closed when a hand cupped her breast. Her nipple eagerly pressed into Erica's palm, the second hand cupped the other breast, and Tasha's knees buckled.

"Open your eyes." Erica's voice rang out an octave lower.

Tasha's eyes fluttered open as she grabbed Erica's waist for stability. Desire was weakening her. Her eyes stared into eyes that promised passion.

"Remove my jacket, tie and shirt while I enjoy these swollen nipples between my fingers."

"Can we go to the bedroom?" Tasha asked.

"Lead the way," Erica responded.

Tasha went to turn, but the pinch on her nipples tightened. She would need to walk backward because Erica had no plan of letting go of her nipples. Erica followed her step by step. Their lips touched in a slow, deep kiss before tongues swirled in rhythm while thumbs rolled the tight buds around in small circles. The closer they got to the bedroom, the harder it was for Tasha to concentrate on kissing. She untangled the knot of the blue airways tie and dropped it to the floor. The jacket joined the tie, then the shirt. Tasha twisted the hooks, and the bra fell free. Her hands found a small breast waiting for her touch. A deep moan escaped Erica and filled Tasha's mouth.

"Perfect," Erica whispered into their kiss. "Now, my belt."

Their kiss broke, and Tasha sat on the bed, looking at the half-naked woman. She slowly unbuckled the belt and then slipped the leather through the belt loops.

"Jeez, you are so hot. Remove the rest." Erica said as she gave each nipple a pull.

Tasha's eyes became heavy, and she moaned out, but she

wasted no time stripping the pilot down. Her nipples were on fire, and she longed for them to be licked and sucked—a small mound lay inches from her lips and smells of arousal teased her senses.

"Take your hand and spread me, then lick me all over," Erica ordered.

Tasha spread the lips to the sweet-smelling pussy, and her tongue rolled around the hardened clit. She pulled the hood back and flicked it gently. She got rewarded with a moan and a pull of her nipple.

Through heavy breaths, Erica moaned her words. "All over, please."

Tasha's tongue rolled over the folds, back up to the clit before she sucked gently, then trailed back down; her tongue circled the wet hole in a tease. Juices dripped into her mouth, and she craved more. Tasha grabbed Erica's ass and pulled her close. Her fingers dug into her behind as her tongue fucked her. In. Out. She twisted inside her and licked over the g-spot.

Erica moaned. "That feels so good. Please, play with my clit with your fingers. Make me come for you."

Tasha slid her hand over Erica's ass and hip, causing Erica to spread her legs wider. Two fingers pushed down on the throbbing clit.

"Yes," Erica said as a hand finally let go of one of Tasha's nipples and found its way to the back of Tasha's head. "You are so good. Please, make me come."

Tasha moaned into her pussy at the thought, causing Erica to thrust faster. Tasha slipped her tongue quickly inside. She eased out from her and circled the tip of her tongue around the edges of her hole, then through the folds; she rubbed the hard bud up and down with two fingers as it stiffened. Erica pulled harder on Tasha's nipple. Her nipple swelled and stung with pleasure. Tasha pulled her tongue out and her fingers away before leaning back.

Erica looked down. Her chest expanded with each heavy breath. "I was so close. Is something wrong?"

A smile crossed Tasha's face. Without a word, she slipped two fingers deep into the tight pussy. She watched as Erica's head fell back and her eyes closed. She started fucking her slowly. Fingers and hips moved in a dance. Tasha reached up with her free hand and played with the large cherry-colored nipple between her fingers. Erica was peaking.

"AH!"

"Yes, you are ready to come for me. You are so wet and tight."

"Suck my clit." Erica pleaded.

Tasha leaned over and sucked on the bud, causing Erica to buck as her insides tightened around Tasha's two fingers. Erica fell over the edge of an orgasm as she released Tasha's nipple and grasped at her shoulders. She groaned deeply from her belly. "Tasha, oh. I'm coming. Oh yes. Now."

Tasha flicked her tongue while sucking on the wetness. Her fingers glistened as she dragged them from Erica's warmth before rolling the tip of her finger over the sensitive bud peeking from its hood. Tasha felt the aftershock hit Erica as she screamed her name before releasing again. Erica fell to her knees with her head landing on Tasha's lap. Tasha stroked through the blonde strands of hair until Erica's breathing slowed.

"Fuck, woman," Erica mumbled. She raised her face, bringing their eyes to a meet. "My turn to please you"

Erica's tongue trailed inside Tasha's thigh, and a shiver of pleasure shot through her body. She moaned when two fingers parted her swollen pink lips, causing her knees to fall apart.

Leaning back on her arms with elbows locked, Tasha watched as a tongue licked her length.

She lifted her hips and moaned at the delicious sight before her. She was wet and ready. After feasting on Erica, her juices flowed, her clit swollen, her nipples stung, and her entire body was on fire. "That feels so good."

"You are so wet. Did I make you this way?"

"Yes," Tasha moaned the word out.

Tasha felt the absence of the mouth on her wet pussy, and she looked down to find Erica climbing her body. She stops at her swollen, throbbing nipples. "Please, take them in your mouth. " Red lips engulf them, and Tasha screamed her pleasure.

"Do you think if I sat here between your legs and sucked only on your nipples, I can make you come?" Erica pulled the bud with her teeth. "Without touching your clit or driving my fingers deep inside you."

"I want it all." The words barely escaped between heavy breaths.

Erica rolled her tongue around the nipple. "You want this?"

"Yes," Tasha moaned.

Erica sucked it in between her lips. "And this?"

"Oh, yes,"

A fingertip slipped quickly between folds and teased the needing clit that pulsated between Tasha's legs.

"And you want this?" Erica asked.

"Oh, oh, yes."

Two fingers passed her entry, and Tasha thought she would explode. They buried deep in her.

"By your tightness, I take it you want this?" Erica breathed the words over Tasha's breast.

Tasha bucked against the fingers deep inside. She would not last as need surfaced deep from her belly with an explosion teetering on the edge. "Faster. Make me come. I got so horny eating you. Please."

The fingers slipped in and out with ease. Tasha looked down as small lips sucked her right nipple, pulling it to its limit. A thumb rolled over her clit, and electricity shot through her body. In, out, oh, she was going to come. Her hips moved in a quick thrust motion as she tightened. She was there.

"Can I come?"

Erica let the nipple pop from her mouth. Their eyes met. "Come for me."

Tasha fell over the edge. She rode those fingers hard like a prize bull, allowing them to come to the edge of her entry and thrust deep back inside. A primal grunt escaped.

"Yes, yes. OH...oh...oh..."

Erica made sure Tasha released every drop of sweet nectar. Tasha grabbed the wrist and pulled the wet fingers from her throbbing insides. "Oh my god." Her elbows folded, and she collapsed on the bed. She couldn't take anymore.

A few minutes slipped by, and the both of them laid curled on the bed, arms and legs intertwined. Time was clicking away, and they knew the bliss would soon end.

"This was amazing," Erica said.

"Yes, it has been," Tasha answered.

"I've got to get back to the airport. I wanted to ask you." Erica pushed a strand of hair from Tasha's face. "I'm going to be back in town in three weeks. I've got a four-day layover. Would you like to see each other again?"

Tasha pushed up on one elbow. "I can't think of a better way to spend four days than with you." She kissed Erica's cheek and rolled her body over hers into a stand before pulling Erica up.

"I don't want you to be late for the flight. Come on. Let's find your uniform."

Ten minutes later, Erica leaned against the same door frame in her sexy pilot's uniform. Tasha slipped a piece of paper into her hand. "My phone number."

"I'll call you soon. Thank you, Tasha."

Their lips hovered inches apart in a promised kiss as they both whispered,

"Until the next delay."

ABOUT THE AUTHOR

LL Shelton is a sapphic literature author. She enjoys writing multiple genres, that include, but not limited to, erotica, contemporary romance, and paranormal romance. The reader will find strong woman characters with flaws in her books that allows a love/hate relationship to develop between the reader and characters.

- Facebook: https://www.facebook.com/author.llshelton

UNDER HER SPELL

RAVEN J. SPENCER

When Emmy walked down the stairs to the lobby and past the small crowd to the private bar area, the room erupted in cheers.

"Thank you! Have a great night!" She waved to them but didn't stop. None of the fans assembled tried to interrupt her. She had come down earlier to talk to a few of them, take pictures and sign autographs.

Around one a.m., the thrill of a successful show still made her body tingle all over, but she was looking for somewhere more relaxed and quieter to unwind. The hotel bar was the perfect place. Most of the tables were occupied, but the generous space made it feel intimate. Muted colors and dimmed lights set the tone.

She sat on a barstool and studied the menu, a friendly but discreet bartender waiting for her order.

Emmy contemplated having a glass or two of expensive champagne. She had earned it, and not just because she had made commanding an audience of thirty-thousand look effortless.

The exhilaration had stayed with her. The night was still young.

"Hello Emmy. Mind if I join you?"

Emmy's breath caught in her throat when she turned to the woman who had asked the question. Her warm, sensual tone revealed her confidence in what she expected the answer to be.

Emmy had dressed in skinny jeans and a top with a plunging neckline after her shower. She could get away with the almost casual gear. Hotel employees knew who she was, and that she was the reason for the fans gathering in the lobby and ordering drinks and food tonight.

The other woman's dress was more appropriate for the setting, short enough to reveal long legs accentuated by high heels. The silky, dark blue fabric seemed to be caressing her curves.

Emmy couldn't fight the image of her doing just that. Within a heartbeat, the air was ripe with promise.

"I don't mind, if you have a glass of champagne with me."

That earned her a smile.

"This was easier than I thought, to be honest. Yes, I'd love to. You were amazing tonight."

"Thank you."

They held each other's gaze while the bartender opened the bottle and filled their glasses. Any residual fatigue had vanished in the wake of excitement, the warmth spreading through her body quickly turning into desire. Familiar, and yet...not.

They lightly clinked their glasses together.

"To a great night."

Emmy couldn't agree more, especially when she saw her own emotions reflected in the other woman's eyes. She might give up all pretense in a heartbeat or two. She couldn't wait for the inevitable outcome...but there was a role to play for each of them. The rock star. The #1 fan.

She searched her feverish mind for something eloquent to say, some clever small talk, but all she could think of was *Would you like to go upstairs?*

She reined in the impulse. That would be too lackluster, and this was the last thing Emmy wanted tonight.

"So, you liked the show? What was your favorite part?"

"I like you," the woman clarified. "But that part where you come down in a trapeze looks amazing. Sexy...and dangerous at the same time."

"It's not that dangerous, I have to admit..." Reveling in the flattery, she wasn't going to admit that she hadn't been all that comfortable with the idea at first. "I'm glad you enjoyed yourself." She took a sip and set her glass on the counter. They were sitting so close their knees almost touched. Emmy reached out to lay her hand on the woman's exposed thigh, nearly sighing with relief at the feel of warm skin under her fingertips. She had to remind herself that they were still in public.

"Oh, I did. And I was wondering...if I could do something for you in return."

The heat between them was tangible, spiking with their imagination running wild, and breathless anticipation.

"Really? What did you have in mind?"

She got an enigmatic smile in return.

"How about we go somewhere more private, and I'll show you?"

Emmy's words came out in a rasp as she slipped off the barstool.

"That's an excellent idea."

Every step reminded her of her state of need as they walked across the bar and to the elevators. Emmy didn't dare look at her, or her own reflection in the mirror. She might not be able to control herself. She focused on the feel of the hand in hers, a hand that would soon take liberties touching her. Emmy had always been blessed with a vivid imagination.

Her hand shook as she opened the room to her suite with her key card.

"That's impressive. You have impeccable taste."

"Thanks. I assume you include yourself in that...and you're right to do so."

She nearly sagged in relief when they kissed, bodies pressing against one another, and the hands pulling her closer promising a release before long. Fingertips brushed over the fabric of her shirt, her nipples perking under the careful touch.

Trying something wild, something she'd never done before, had ended badly for her one time, at least temporarily. This was different. Safe.

Barely breaking the kiss, they removed each other's clothing, making their way to the king-size bed. Emmy shivered as she lay back in the cool sheets, taking pleasure in all the ways her body was caressed, explored, worshiped.

Her gasps turned into moans soon stifled by the hot mouth on hers. Out there, on stage, she was in complete control. She could lose herself in the music and the words, but she never lost the command of the audience. In this room, she was powerless, and she loved every moment of it.

Her hips rose, the warm pressure of fingertips against her clit intensifying, fingers moving faster against her, then inside her...She was ready. Her partner didn't think so, and Emmy didn't hold back the frustrated sound when the desired touch vanished.

"You can't be serious." Her tone reflected clearly how close she was...had been. "Come on."

"Trust me. You won't regret it. I promise."

How could she resist that confident smile? Emmy sighed, willing herself to be patient while her body demanded release. She allowed her legs to be parted by those curious hands, her breath catching in her throat when soft lips touched against the inside of her thigh.

"Please," she murmured, her hands reaching out to tangle in soft strands of hair. She basked in the familiar, hedonistic feel of a warm tongue exploring her, taking her onto the path to a mind-shattering climax. Emmy couldn't hold back the whimper. It sounded slightly pathetic to her ears, but she was long past caring. Past the moment of no return.

She could feel her eyes well up with the first stirrings of her orgasm, reveling in the unreal experience, the full-blown glory of it leaving her breathless.

After taking a few seconds to catch her breath, Andrea moved up on the bed to lie next to her and pull her into her arms. Still trembling, Emmy smiled against her chest.

"You are so intense," Andrea whispered. "I've always loved that about you."

"Always?"

"From the moment we met. Even though you could be challenging. In a good way," she added so quickly Emmy had to laugh, still a little breathless.

"I can imagine. So...how did you like it?" Emmy asked, curious. The idea that Andrea was reminiscing about those past moments did nothing to calm her heart rate.

"It was a bit strange," Andrea admitted, "but so hot. I think we both know how to stay in character. It's just different in this context."

"I know what you mean. I would have liked to play a bit longer...but I couldn't stop myself. Anyway. I could never imagine inviting a groupie to my hotel room."

"Until now." Andrea was amused.

"Only when she's also my wife," Emmy clarified.

"I wasn't kidding earlier. You were amazing. The way you do it...It does turn me on."

The praise warmed her cheeks and other places. Emmy was used to praise, some of it with sexual undertones...This was different. Much as they had tried in the beginning, neither of them had been able to ignore the out-of-bounds chemistry between them.

"I'm glad you think so."

"I do," Andrea confirmed as Emmy pulled back to move on top of her in one swift move.

With satisfaction, she noticed the way Andrea's eyes darkened with desire. She couldn't ignore the hint of surprise.

"What? You didn't think I'd repay the favor?"

"You're the rock star," Andrea returned. "It's all up to you... I think?"

They both laughed, until Emmy pinned her wrists above her head and leaned in for a deep, breathless kiss.

"That's right. And what I want right now..." She traced her fingers down Andrea's chest and over her stomach, feeling the muscles quiver as her body reacted to the caress, "Is to make you feel good."

"Sounds a bit corny, but I'm with you..." Andrea's cheeky comment ended in a gasp when Emmy slid a hand between her legs.

She wasted no time, thrilled to know exactly what she needed to do to prolong the moment, finding a rhythm that would keep Andrea on the edge until Emmy decided it was time.

Being in control...She liked that too. Andrea yielded to her efforts easily.

They fell asleep in each other's arms, and that was part of the plan too.

Always.

Andrea woke with a smile on her face, as she remembered vague but thrilling dreams in which their play continued. Her reality was even more exciting than just dreaming about Emmy Whittaker, the way she had when it seemed impossible that they could ever be together—the way many fans did.

She pushed back the sheets and reached for her robe, watching Emmy who was sitting in an armchair by the window, wearing a tank top and short PJ pants. Emmy was writing on a notepad, completely focused on her task. After tying the belt of her robe, Andrea walked over to her. She realized it was only 5.00 a.m., but like Emmy, she felt wide awake.

And hungry.

"I hope this means I inspired you."

"Always." Emmy looked up and gave her a quick smile. "In fact, I'm almost done, and since you're awake..."

Exciting didn't even begin to cover it. She had slept for a few hours, and they still had time before they had to go to the airport.

"Absolutely," she said, feeling her body react to the memory and promise of more unbelievable pleasure.

"I was thinking about ordering a cheeseburger...the truffles and champagne that came with the room are nice, but I'm so hungry..." Emmy started laughing. "That's not what you were thinking about, was it?"

"You got me there, but food does sound nice," Andrea admitted. "I came right to the hotel earlier."

"And we didn't waste any time." Emmy picked up the phone. "What would you like?"

"Same as you is fine."

"Great. I'm on it."

When Emmy was on the phone with room service, Andrea couldn't help glancing at the words on paper...*Under Her Spell*. It made her smile. Her decision to be with Emmy had come with sacrifices, but she didn't regret a single one of them. Before, she had no idea how happy she could be. Andrea was learning, every day.

"Okay, late dinner or early breakfast coming right up. What's wrong?" Emmy asked, sounding worried.

"Nothing. It's actually perfect. I love you so much."

"I love you too. And I'm so happy you came..." She halted, realizing how words could be interpreted in different ways.

"Me too," Andrea returned, amused at the truth in their exchange. No matter the interpretation.

When their food arrived, they took it to the sitting area next to the huge window. Andrea wasn't sure if that had been part of the groupie fantasy. Having room service in a luxury hotel in the early morning hours was certainly fit for a rock star. *Her* rock star.

She glanced over at Emmy and smiled. As long as she was with her, every day would be an adventure.

If you enjoyed this story, you can find more of Emmy and Andrea in *On The Record*, Book One in the *Love In The Limelight* series: smarturl.it/OnTheRecordbyRJS

ABOUT THE AUTHOR

Raven J. Spencer, lesbian, married, loves everything sensual and indulgent. When she's not writing, you can often find her on Pinterest in the pursuit of inspiration and cheesecake recipes.

Her works include the Love In The Limelight series (celebrity romance), the Surrender series (billionaire romance with a suspense twist), and several standalone titles.

- Website: http://ravenspencer.blogspot.com/

- Facebook: https://www.facebook.com/RavenJSpencer

WORK WEEK

KC LUCK

Wednesday

Gillian grabbed a handful of the taller woman's curly brown hair and pulled her down until their lips crashed together. The sexy butch's kisses were hot, and the feel of her tongue in her mouth was thrilling, but she already felt the need for her to focus that caress elsewhere. Or, more distinctly, to bury her gorgeous face in Gillian's ever increasingly wet pussy. "I want you to fuck me with your tongue," she murmured, and with her fingers still entwined in the woman's hair, Gillian guided Max's head. She obeyed without comment and, after sliding to her knees, allowed herself to be steered between Gillian's legs. Feeling Max's hot breath against her lacy panties, Gillian moved herself a little closer to the edge of the desk and slipped one of her legs over the woman's shoulder. It was going to feel good, and she knew it. She'd had been thinking about the courier delivery woman for too long, and if her lush lips and wicked little smile weren't up to the challenge of getting Gillian off, no one's could.

"Pull my panties to the side," Gillian ordered. She felt one of Max's fingers slip under the edge of the silky fabric between her legs. It brushed her swollen lips and sent a shock of excitement through her. Sensing her reaction, the woman slid her finger slowly up and down, pausing to roll the tip over her clit. Gillian closed her eyes. It felt fantastic. "Now kiss me there," she said, expecting to be obeyed without question. It was all she allowed from her lovers—complete compliance or nothing. The butch didn't hesitate. Pulling the panties to the side, Max leaned closer and used her lips to suck Gillian's swollen clit into her hot mouth.

Unable to help herself, Gillian arched her back at the exquisite sensation, pressing her mouth harder against the woman's face. She felt the tip of her tongue gently explore her swollen lips and dip down to tease her opening. "Deeper," Gillian said, her breath coming faster. There was no time to waste. Her next appointment with a client was in ten minutes.

A sudden shift in her partner's body brought Gillian back to focus on the moment. She felt the woman's other hand start to slide up her thigh. Tentatively, she stopped just beneath her chin and waited. Gillian considered her silent proposal. She had not been finger fucked in ages, but was there time? Oh, screw it, she thought and tilted her head back. "Do it," she said with conviction. "Two fingers. I want it tight." With her mouth still on Gillian's clit, the delivery woman immediately slipped the tips of her fingers past the edge of her pussy. Gillian felt herself being spread apart, and she loved it. "More," she said and moaned when the woman's hand pushed harder, sliding over the ridges at the top of her opening. Any second, she would be at Gillian's g-spot. "Oh God," she murmured. An orgasm was building, and it threatened to be a big one.

Moving faster, the woman inside her sucked and stroked, bumping the g-spot with each thrust of her hand. Gillian bit her lip, knowing crying out was not an option. But it was going to be hard to stay quiet. It had been weeks since she came, and her body's pent-up desire was about to spill over onto the desk. "Don't stop," Gillian said with a moan. "Make me come. Make me come." Suddenly, the sensation of the woman's fingers grew tighter, and she realized she had slipped a third finger into her. The extra pressure was exactly what she needed. Feeling her muscles tighten, her body grabbed at the woman's deep fingers and felt the heat begin to spread from between her legs and through her body. Ripples of passion rolled over her, and she dug her high heel into the delivery woman's back, pulling Max tight against her as she came hard.

Monday, two days before

Tapping her limited-edition Mont Blanc pen on the top of her expansive glass-topped desk, Gillian went through the calculations one last time in her head. The merger would be life-changing, not only for her, but for thousands of employees around the globe. Wall Street held its breath, waiting to see what the great Gillian Verde would do. Her legal team had scoured the contract to ensure every T was crossed and every I was dotted. All she had left was to go with her gut. A business degree from Harvard University helped her make calculated decisions, but in the end, with situations like these, it came down to her instinct.

Finally, while her executive assistant and two lawyers from the other corporations waited, smart enough to hardly breathe, Gillian signed the dotted line. Not surprised, she heard the three of them exhale. The deal was done. Of course, adjustments were always made as part of a colossal merger, but the impetus to start the dominos was completed. "I need a minute," Gillian said, feeling her usual sense of accomplishment at making a good business decision. Only that signature was the biggest of her life. Unable to help it, the power made her feel slightly aroused, and being alone in her giant corner office was all she wanted. That and some big butch stud to come fuck her as she felt her hundred-dollar lace panties grow wet. But alas, one of the sacrifices of running the world was isolation. As they said, it was lonely at the top.

As the trio left with the documents, but otherwise not a word, Gillian turned her chair to face the floor-to-ceiling windows that looked over Seattle. Rain ran down them, as was almost always the case in November in the Pacific Northwest. Still, Gillian didn't mind it. She loved the Emerald City for all its lush vibrancy. She thought that maybe a night on the town was in order. A celebration, although it was only Monday. All it would take was a couple of phone calls to bring her friends together, and her executive assistant could make the last-minute reservation.

Deciding that was the right course of action, she buzzed her assistant, sitting at a desk right outside her office door. There was a pause, unusually long, and to the point Gillian frowned. Her executive assistant had been with her for years and would never make the mistake of letting a page go unanswered. She was about to try again when the woman picked up the line. "I apologize, Ms. Verde. What did you need?"

Before Gillian could say a word, she heard a voice over the speaker. It was deep, but still a trace feminine. "I don't have time for this," the woman said. "All it takes is a signature." The image that popped into Gillian's head went straight to her fantasies. Already feeling a bit of an ache in much need of release, she rolled the dice. Of course, the woman so eager to come in could look a world apart from Gillian's fantasy, but for some reason, the instinct that always rang true guided her.

"Let her come in," Gillian said into the intercom. After a moment, the door to her office opened. Her executive assistant held it, and for a beat, Gillian could not see the stranger. Then, as if an answer from the gods, the delivery woman appeared. She filled the doorway with her broad shoulders and, although not tall, made up for it with her powerful presence. Short brown curly hair offset a pair of snapping blue eyes. The woman was clearly not happy at being delayed. Striding past the executive assistant, she approached the desk with a letter-sized manila envelope in one hand and a device Gillian recognized she was supposed to sign. If Gillian had a fantasy lover in mind, the delivery woman far surpassed it.

Unable to help herself, Gillian licked her lips as the

stranger stopped at the edge of her desk. "Ms. Gillian Verde?" she asked.

Gillian nodded. "Yes," she said, her voice pitched a little huskier than usual. "What do you have for me?"

A smile played across the delivery woman's mouth, as if sensing the question was loaded with innuendo. "Nothing but a letter... tonight," she answered, her tone deep and confident. "Were you expecting something more?"

A glance at her executive assistant still at the door brought Gillian back to her senses. Undoubtedly for the best, considering how very much she wanted the courier on her knees between her legs. "No," she replied. "I wasn't expecting you. Where is Thomas, our usual delivery man?"

"Out for a few days," the stranger said. "I'm filling in until he's back."

A throb at the idea she might see the delectable specimen of a woman again sent a small thrill through her. "I see," Gillian said. "Well, I hope he is okay. And what is your name?"

"Max."

"Of course it is," Gillian murmured. "Where do I need to sign?"

Tuesday

As much as she would never admit it, all day Gillian had not stopped thinking lustful thoughts about the sexy woman named Max who had made the delivery the day before. Staring out her high-rise office window, unusually distracted from the many tasks still left on her to-do list, Gillian tried to determine what had her so turned on. Something about the confidence in the woman's brown eyes and the way she carried herself as she strode across the room excited her. If she had met Max at a high-end bar or a club, Gillian would have made it her mission to get her into bed. But that was not the case, and there was a strong possibility they would never come face to face again. For Gillian, that was simply unacceptable.

Spinning in her chair, she faced her oversized desk, wondering how she could arrange for Max to come back. A pulse of anticipation started between her legs at the thought, making her cross them under her pencil skirt to help lessen it. She could feel the wet heat inside her panties, and it was all she could do not to squirm. The problem had to be addressed.

Her executive assistant handled any courier-related details, so Gillian wasn't sure how to contact the delivery company. All her lusting might be for naught if the wrong courier arrived. It had to be the same as yesterday. Of course, it crossed Gillian's mind that the woman might not be prepared for what she wanted, but in her mind, it needed to be explored. The chemistry was strong, and a sexual tension had hung in the air throughout the entire exchange. Although Gillian would never use her power and insist the butch please her, she somehow knew Max wanted to fuck her. Gillian was sure of it, and her killer instincts were never wrong.

Unable to wait, she elected to put the wheels in motion and reached for the intercom. Unlike the day before, her assistant answered the buzz in only a second. "Yes, Ms. Verde?" Gillian opened her mouth, ready to ask about the delivery service, but then stopped. She wasn't sure how to frame her question—*do you happen to know if that sexy, broad-shouldered butch would be back today?* Seemed a little too obvious. Clearing her throat, she started over. "I wondered if you could arrange for a courier pick up," she said. "I have a follow up to the contract from yesterday that I would like delivered as soon as possible."

"Oh," her executive assistant. "I'm sorry, I didn't know—"

"I took care of everything," Gillian interrupted, closing her eyes. The request sounded more and more unbelievable every second. "I just need someone to pick it up."

"Yes, Ms. Verde. It is after hours, though," her executive assistant explained. "I will have to use a specialty service." Surprised, Gillian looked at the clock. Amazingly, it was after five o'clock. Typically, her assistant would be leaving any second. "Unless you want me to drop it off."

Gillian cursed to herself. "No," she said. "But first thing in the morning. It can't wait much longer."

The start of Wednesday

Minutes ticked by, and Gillian's frustration grew. Arriving early, she made it clear to her executive assistant that when the delivery woman arrived, to send her in. "But, Ms. Verde, if you prefer, I can hold the—"

"No," Gillian all but snapped. "I want to hand it over personally." That was an hour ago, and she was about to buzz her assistant again when there was a tap at the door. Puzzled because her assistant would never knock without using the intercom first, Gillian considered ignoring it, but then the idea struck her—Max. "Come in."

As if right out of her fantasies, the door opened to reveal the woman Gillian could not stop thinking about. "Sorry, but there's no one out here, and I was told the pickup was urgent," Max said, stepping into the office.

Gillian stood from her desk, moving around it to ensure there was nothing between them. "Oh, it is very urgent."

"I see," Max said, a smile playing on her lips. "Well, when I saw the address for the delivery, I made a point of taking it myself." She paused as she took a step closer. "Just in case."

Feeling heat bloom between her legs at the confirmation

Max wanted her, Gillian leaned against the edge of the desk. "Mmm," she hummed. "Please lock the door."

Thursday

Sitting at her desk, Gillian glanced at her phone to check the hour for the hundredth time. The workday could not have possibly moved slower, making Gillian a little crazy. Everyone paid the price of her impatience, and she snapped at anyone who dared cross her path. Even though the day before she had possibly the best orgasm of her life, it did not relax her. Anticipation had her on the edge of her seat, and the sensation of wearing nothing under her skirt bothered her in all the most erotic ways. Nonstop images of Max on top of her kept her clit tight, and more than once, she contemplated going to her private bathroom to get herself off. Only the thought of how much harder she would come if she waited made her behave.

Finally, her executive assistant buzzed her intercom. "Yes," Gillian answered, her voice breathless with anticipation.

"I'm leaving for the night, Ms. Verde," her assistant said. "Unless you need something else." A wave of near panic washed through Gillian as she looked at the time. Well after five o'clock and no visit from Max. That's not possible, she thought. She had been convinced the woman knew Gillian wanted her again.

Gillian pushed the intercom. "Were there any deliveries today?" she asked, aware it was a weird question but needed to hear.

There was a pause, and then the assistant answered. "Yes, there were," she said. "Thomas is back."

No, Gillian wanted to scream but instead told the assistant goodbye. "I can't believe this has happened," she whispered to the empty office, trying to decide what to do next. She had no idea how to reach Max other than through the delivery company, and that felt desperate. Facing the reality, all her aching was for nothing, Gillian reached for the small vibrator she had hidden in her purse in case they wanted to play with it today. If Max didn't want to please her, Gillian would take care of herself. Turning it on, Gillian slid up her skirt until she had access to her throbbing clit. Even in her frustration, she knew she would come fast. A moment before touching herself, there was a soft knock at her office door. She froze. Things were about to be awkward or wonderful; she wasn't sure. "Who is it?" she asked, and the voice she had been fantasizing about all day answered.

"Max," she said. "May I come in?"

Turning off the vibrator and stuffing it in her purse again, Gillian shrugged down her skirt before standing. "Please do," she finally said, and the door opened to reveal Max. Not in her delivery clothes though, but a fitted, sexy black t-shirt and tight jeans that showed off the narrowness of her hips. And possibly something else. As Gillian's eyes took in the slight bulge in Max's pants, she felt her pussy spread open in anticipation.

Max locked the door without being asked. "Sorry I took all day," she said, walking toward Gillian. "But I wanted us to meet when I wasn't on the clock. Does that disappoint you?"

"Not at all," Gillian said, meaning the words. The attraction to Max was never about some kinky fantasy to fuck a delivery woman. "I love how you look in your clothes." She licked her lips as her eyes flicked to the shape of something in Max's tight jeans.

Max chuckled, clearly full of confidence. "I thought you might."

Suddenly, Gillian wasn't entirely sure she liked the change in roles. Although she wasn't using her power to force Max to have sex with her, she did want to remain in charge of what happened between them. Her pace. Her decisions. Strap-on or no strap-on.

She nodded toward the couch that filled the sitting area in her office. "Sit down," she said, and was happy to see Max do what she instructed. Gillian went to join her and loved the feel of the cool leather against her bare legs. Having sex on the thing never crossed her mind until tonight, but straddling Max seemed a perfect way to stay in control. Still, as she turned to look at her, their eyes met, and the sultry look of the delivery woman had changed to something deeper.

It was almost like she had turned on some sort of charm. No, not charm, Gillian thought. Something more animal, and it spoke right to Gillian's core. She looked into her eyes and knew without any doubt Max wanted her. Right there, right now. She felt herself suddenly grow even hotter and wetter between her legs.

As if sensing her desire, she watched as Max slowly leaned toward her. Their faces were only an inch apart. For the briefest moment, Gillian wondered if the new intimacy forming between them was a bad idea. Unexpected emotions raged in her. One part wanted the kiss almost desperately, while the other worried it was a mistake. Max decided for her and closed the distance to put her lips against Gillian's. She could not help but lean in. Unlike the frantic kiss the day before, this time Max's mouth was soft but strong, and when she tickled Gillian's tongue with her own, sparks of desire ran through Gillian. Not wanting to hold back now, she held the kiss and reached forward to press on the bulge in her jeans. Knowing the pressure would rub on Max's clit, Gillian loved the reward of her moaning deep in her throat. With hands stronger than she would have imagined, Max grabbed her by the hips and started to pull her onto her lap.

Immediately, Gillian tensed. She was not about to let Max

make that decision. Things would go at her pace or not at all. Breaking the kiss, Gillian pushed Max's hands away. "Wait," she said breathlessly. "Let me do it." Max dropped her hands and let Gillian slide up her skirt before stretching a leg over Max's hips. Settling down so her wet pussy brushed against the friction of Max's jeans, it was all she could do not to gasp. But if she wanted to run the show, things needed to slow down.

Beginning to unbutton her blouse, Gillian let a smile play over her lips as she revealed her lacy black bra. "Now behave," she said in a sensual tone. "And I'll tell you what I want." Max licked her lips, and Gillian felt her confidence returning. She ran her hand back over the bulge again. "Take it out," she instructed. Max, holding her gaze, reached for her belt, but then paused.

"No, you do it," she said softly, but with a hint of rebelliousness. Gillian paused and studied her face. God, she is so gorgeous, she thought, but there was more to it. Her eyes held a depth that warned of complexities Gillian was sure she did not need in her life. Thinking perhaps things were best left unfinished, she started to slide back off when Max slipped her hands under the edge of Gillian's skirt and caressed her thighs. Gillian bit her lip. Max's hands were strong and hot against her skin, and she could not help but think about the strap-on and how much she ached to feel it. Still, Gillian did not like her refusal. It was time to take back control. She grabbed Max's hands, pulling them to her breasts. Max did not disappoint and cupped them in her palms, rubbing her thumbs over the fabric straining across her nipples. Gillian arched her back and moaned with pleasure. That was more like it. She ran her hands along Max's arms and felt the thickness of her biceps. So powerful. So strong. She wanted her badly, and grinding her hips against her jeans, Gillian heard Max's breath catch.

"I want to feel you inside me," Gillian murmured and felt

Max slightly lift her hips. She knew she must be aching to fuck her, too.

"Not yet," Max said in a whisper, and lowered her lips to the spot between Gillian's breasts. She felt her hot lips caress the skin. In response, Gillian ground her hips harder, and the barrier between them was driving her crazy.

Max slid her mouth up to her neck and slipped her hands around Gillian to pull her down tighter against her lap. The movement rocked her hips, and Gillian felt the rough fabric of her jeans touch her hard clit again. The sensation was electric, and Gillian cried out softly. She did not know how much more of the teasing she could take. She wanted to feel Max filling her up and thrusting inside her. "What are you waiting for?" she moaned.

In answer, Max took Gillian's slender hands in hers and guided them to her belt buckle. Her unspoken message was clear. Let the strap-on out, and she would give Gillian what she needed. Mixed emotions raged through her. Such a simple thing, unhooking her pants, yet it would mean giving in. Should she do it? As if to finally convince her, Max let go of her hands, leaving them at her belt, and reached under her skirt to graze her thumb perfectly across Gillian's throbbing clit. That did it. She wasn't waiting any longer. She wanted to be fucked, and right now.

Grabbing Max's buckle, she unhooked it in seconds and pulled at her zipper. Max growled with pleasure as Gillian's hand slipped into the gap and pulled the strap-on shaft out of her jeans. "Oh yes," Gillian moaned. The strap-on was fantastic. Thick in her grasp and at least eight inches, Gillian did not hesitate to lift her hips and force it inside her. The tip spread her apart, and Gillian could not believe how good it felt. Before Max pushed even halfway into her, Gillian felt the orgasm coming. All the foreplay and teasing had pulled her to the brink, and now that the strap-on was inside her, she was going to come. Everything was perfect because she knew Max would not be ready yet. It would be payback for her unwillingness to cooperate. Letting the pent-up feeling inside her rage loose, she rode the strap-on for a few strokes and then felt her pussy start to twitch. Closing her eyes and tilting her head back, she squeezed Max's biceps hard with her nails and came.

Relishing the release, she looked into Max's eyes. "Thank you for that," she said, starting to lift off her lap when Max's hands were on her hips. Her grip was strong, and Gillian could not stop her as she pulled her back down. This time, the shaft drove deeper, and Gillian gasped. As Max arched her hips, every part of Gillian was filled, and she cried out with over-whelming pleasure. The sensation was so intense. "You're not really ready to be done, are you?" Max growled mischievously.

"No," she heard herself whimper. "Fuck me, Max. Until I can't stand it." The woman did not hesitate and used her hands on Gillian's hips to hold her in place while she rocked under her, driving in and out. Gillian knew she would come again, but now much, much harder. A giant of an orgasm was cresting, and she gasped for breath. Max's hold on her was fierce, and she knew she could not break away from her even if she wanted. Max was taking her, hard and fast and at her own making, and Gillian was not in control.

"Tell me you want it," Max demanded through clenched teeth as she held back her own orgasm but kept up the pace. "Tell me, or I'll stop." Gillian felt almost felt dizzy she wanted the orgasm so bad. Stopping was not an option.

"I want it. God, how I want it," Gillian moaned. "Don't stop. Please." Max lifted them both off the couch cushion with her thrusts, and Gillian screamed with pleasure. She did not care if anyone left in the building could hear. She was coming, and it was beyond anything she could remember.

At the same moment, Max started to moan with pleasure. "Fuck, I'm coming," she growled. "Fuck yes. You're amazing." At the sound of her voice, knowing Max was getting off too, Gillian screamed again as a second wave of throbbing rolled over her. The orgasm went on and on until every ounce of Gillian's strength was gone, and she collapsed onto Max.

Friday

Once again, Gillian sat at her desk, staring out the window as the rain ran down the glass. Although it was only nine a.m., she had canceled all her appointments, realizing she was worthless at business today. The tingle between her legs, reminding her of where Max and her strap-on had been the night before, was too distracting. She had never come like that, and when Gillian was limp on the couch, entirely spent, Max had kissed her on the forehead and left. As amazing as it was, Gillian knew the connection could likely be her worst nightmare. Not because of anything Max might do, but the opposite. Gillian wanted to see the woman again, but had no control over the situation. It's time to break things off, she thought, turning her chair to reach for the intercom.

"Yes, Ms. Verde?" her executive assistant asked.

Gillian hesitated, a part of her longing to see Max again so much she ached, but the woman hadn't even left a phone number. It gave her too much power, which was all the more reason to remove herself from the equation. "I'm leaving for the day," she said. "And I won't be back in the office until Monday."

"Oh, okay," her assistant said, sounding more than a little surprised. "Is something wrong?"

"Everything is fine," Gillian answered a little too quickly. "I just want to get away for a couple of days." The idea grew on her quickly. A little time to relax and let the idea of Max work its way out of her system. The message would be clear enough when the woman couldn't reach Gillian. After locking her desk drawers and gathering her purse, she made her way out of the office, pausing at her assistant's desk. "Please let anyone looking for me know I'm unavailable until Monday morning."

The woman nodded, clearly unsure of what to make of Gillian leaving so suddenly. Smiling with satisfaction that she had taken care of the situation, Gillian started for the elevators. "Oh, wait, Ms. Verde," the assistant said. "There's an envelope here for you. I meant to bring it in a second before you buzzed me."

Gillian turned to look at her. "From where?" she asked, unable to ignore the flutter of excitement in her stomach.

Turning the small white envelope over, her assistant frowned. "I think the thing was here this morning when I arrived, but there's no return information," she said. "All it has is your name." She looked at Gillian. "Do you want me to open it?"

"No," Gillian snapped before catching herself. "I mean, no thank you. I will take the envelope."

"Yes, Ms. Verde," the assistant said, handing it over. The impulse to tear it open on the spot was strong, but Gillian forced herself to wait at least until she was alone in the elevator. With shaking hands, she opened the envelope to find a slip of paper. The note was from Max, with a phone number, and reading the message, Gillian smiled as her resolve disappeared like a wisp of smoke. "If you liked the work week," the words said. "Let me show you what I can do on the weekend."

ABOUT THE AUTHOR

KC Luck is a bestselling author of sapphic fiction. Writing is her passion, and nothing energizes her more than creating new characters facing trials and tribulations in a complex plot. Whether it is an apocalypse, contemporary romance, or something a little naughty with every story KC tries to add her own unique twist. KC Luck is active in the LGBTQ+ community and the founder of the self-published author collective iReadIndies.

- Website: https://www.kc-luck.com/index.html

- Facebook: https://www.facebook.com/kc. luckauthor.92/

- Twitter: https://twitter.com/kc_luck_author

- iReadIndies: https://ireadindies.com/index.html

DESIRE AND BRIMSTONE

ALYSON TONG

There were several dozen moments Asha would remember for the rest of her life for their stupidity, their brilliance, and their life changing consequences. And there was the handful that was all of the above. This is the story of the biggest of those moments.

"You've been given a choice, the noose or one last heist. Yeah, some fucking choice." Asha mutters to herself as she scales the side of a tower of a decrepit castle hundreds of years old guarded by a real-life fire-breathing dragon. The tales of the dragon that guarded treasure troves or revered magic had existed as long as anyone knew. Lately, the legend of choice was that someone had entrapped an incredibly beautiful woman in its highest tower. And now the bravest flocked to their deaths to save the mythical woman.

Asha looks up, measuring the distance from her precarious position to the window above her. To be quite frank, she was amazed she hadn't been turned into jerky yet. As she had walked carefully through to the edge of the tree line before the castle cliffs, she had taken note of the verifiable graveyard surrounding the front of it, the majority of bones and varying aged and burnt armor concentrated by the impressive front padlocked doors. Two thoughts had dominated Asha's head at that moment. One, what idiot tried to steal from an ancient, powerful dragon by walking through the front door? And two, what kind of idiot was she for still thinking of how she was going to steal from an ancient, powerful dragon by discovering a hidden back door?

The kind who are caught stealing from the royal treasury and have to either be hung in front of the whole town and her family or be sent on an absolutely impossible quest. She reminds herself.

And so Asha had scoped out the castle for the remainder of

the day and spotted this tower window. Backdoor found. Sure, it was high enough up to make Asha's stomach curdle, but it was a way in. She spent the entire climb thus far ignoring how failure was two out of three options open to her and failure meant drowning in the ocean below or frying to a crisp. So, no other option but to keep climbing. She repeated this in her head over and over until her ragged fingernails caught on the wooden sill of the tower window. She closed her eyes and let out a breath.

"Thanks be to the spirits above and below." She'd made it.

Asha allows herself to smile at her small victory before focusing on getting into the tower room. She has no way of knowing what awaits her when she crosses the threshold. She adjusts her weight so she can pull the knife she has stashed in her boot. She places the gray steel in her mouth and returns her hand to the window's ledge. With a deep breath, she hoists herself as quietly as possible through the open window landing in a crouch inside the tower's room.

Her feet land with hardly a sound and Asha stays in her squat momentarily as she takes in her surroundings. The small open window inlaid at the top of the cliff face tower reveals a single large bedchamber. Embers smolder in a small iron stove, heating the room. On the walls are crooked paintings, as if knocked askew in frustration or out of spite. The ceiling is stained dark black with soot. The smell of something burnt permeates the room. Asha wiggles her nose to keep from sneezing. Dominating the room was a large fourposter bed, curtains drawn around its sides. Two wooden doors on its other side remain closed. Asha takes the blade from her teeth and adjusts her hold as she stands from her low position.

Her limbs stay loose, prepped to defend herself at any moment but with her ears pricked, waiting for the sound of any dragon sized movement. She hears nothing and thinks this room, for now, is safe. And if she had any coin left to gamble, she'd put all of it on there being no fabled maiden she was to steal, sleeping peacefully on the four-poster before her.

On silent feet, Asha slowly makes her way to the frankly out of place and extravagant bed. The gauzy purple curtains that surround the bed reveal a dark silhouette breathing deep and slow, clearly asleep. Asha parted the curtains to see more clearly the woman imprisoned here. And that was why Asha never gambled.

Stretched out on plush pillows under a single silky sheet was the princess of fairy tales. But not as Asha had heard. The woman has deep red hair that fell from the crown of her head down her spine; the ends tickling the curve of her spine before her ass and thighs disappeared beneath the silk. Muted light from the moon outside the window, filtered by the gauzy curtains casts a glow about the woman's skin. She lies on her stomach arms tucked under a pillow beneath her head. Long lashes flutter as she breathes against high, full cheeks. She slept in the warm room, nude. The only thing she adorned was a necklace. A single red gem the size of Asha's palm inlaid on a dark chain around her neck reflects the unfiltered moonlight let in from Asha moving the curtains aside.

Now once a jewel thief, always a jewel thief. And some of those instincts, to inspect, to ascertain the jewel's validity were just parts of Asha now after thieving and selling the spoils of rich assholes as long as she had. Without thinking about it, Asha reaches forward, wanting to tilt the gem in the necklace just a tiny bit further to see how the moonlight filters through, to see the impurities in its formation. But as soon as she touches the jewel, contrary to the ease at which the princess sleeps, and the cool evening air, Asha's fingers are singed, and she pulls back her hand with a muffled yelp. She brings her fingertips to her mouth to suck on the sting before freezing as she realized what she had done.

The figure on the bed stiffens, her face's muscles contracting as consciousness returns. Suddenly, her eyes snap open. Her irises are twin flames lighting the canopied bed with their amber color and unconcealed fury at being awoken.

Asha gasps, stepping back, her foot tangles in the trailing curtains, causing her to stumble and fall to the wooden floor. On her ass, legs splayed before her Asha watches the woman rise from the bed.

The woman pushes herself up seemingly uncaring of her nudity. The gemstone necklace settles in the hollow of her throat as she rises. Her eyes are piercing, and face curls up in a snarl. Her hair falls over her shoulders as she leans forward and two dark shapes rise from her back. Asha's eyes widen as two scaled dark leathery appendages snap out from her shoulder blades. Wings. Her fingers flex revealing rapidly elongating talons. A low rumble fills the space as smoke leaks from the corner of her mouth. Asha feels the blood leave her face as the realization strikes her.

"You're the dragon." She whispers, voice a mere croak, but it seemed the woman heard her all the same over her own growl.

"And you are a thief." The reply echoes with a growl around the tower room.

"No...Err yes! But it's complicated," Asha rushes to explain, scrambling to her knees, "Very complicated." She says under her breath eyes wandering across the wings still fanned out, almost the length of the room itself at their full breadth, they are only half open where the woman stands on her bed.

"I find what you all out there seem to find complicated is really quite simple. You have a desire for the princess. Your desire involves my demise, and you have no qualms about doing what you want to get those desires, throwing everyone and everything to the side to do so, attacking me and my home. Stealing into my bedroom." She doesn't yell but the hissed out accusations burn with rage all the same.

"But I don't want you!" Asha throws out her hands, terrified she will become another skeleton in this princess' literal closet. Or more like a lawn ornament, she supposes. The woman raises a singular brow and straightens thus allowing the moonlight to dance across her body. Under her skin muscles tense and quiver, the princess is standing on the edge, ready to strike if she needs to. Asha averts her eyes, hoping in the dark the heat rushing to her cheeks is not noticed.

"You have snuck into my bedchamber in the middle of the night while I lay prone in my bed, undefended." Asha wants to object. The apparent dragon princess was hardly in danger from a mere mortal like her.

"And you say you don't want me. However, you saw my jewelry and reached for it, a prize perhaps, a trophy. So, if not me, you still have a desire you are risking life and limb for." Asha groans. She tries to think fast. Her eyes dart around the room. She notices see the paintings again. Her head fills with unanswered questions. First and foremost is how to keep this woman talking and get out alive.

"Okay, I will admit I was entranced by the gem in your necklace and moved without thinking. But right now, all I have are questions, many questions." Asha holds up her hands and watches the woman as she cocks her head and begins to consider her. Asha looks behind her and sees one painting in particular that shows a royal family, a tear through the redheaded young girl at its center. A king and a queen and a small crib adorned in jewels is a swaddled thing still asleep. It leans to the side, facing away from the bed. Asha can only see the painting due to her awkward and vulnerable angle from the hard floor. This must be a painting of the princess' family Asha realizes.

"You've been alone a long time. Let's have a chat. You can get to know me and if I don't pass muster, you can barbecue me then. Let me start, I'm Asha. What's your name?" Asha knew she was rambling, but she was hoping her penchant for running her mouth could get her out of one last tight spot. She watches the woman's face as she studies Asha. Her amber eyes narrow and seem to look her over before she steps down from the bed. She crouches over Asha who doesn't dare move a muscle. She feels like she can hardly breathe with the attention of the woman on her. Amber eyes meet her own and they burn with intensity.

"Eden." She breathes, so quietly Asha is almost sure she wasn't meant to hear it. Then the woman straightens.

"My name is Eden. And it has been a very long time since I've had a decent conversation."

"Eden. It's nice to meet you." Asha stumbles over the sentence, feeling relief trickle down her spine like a shock of cold water. She wasn't dying...not yet. Eden turns from her and walks to the other side of the bed. Asha's eyes alight on the wings folding back into Eden's back, tucked lightly against her shoulder blades. From where the two wings enter her back up along her spine to the nape of her neck and then down to the small of her back are a smattering of scales. Dark ruby red they glitter in the low moonlight, bringing attention to the contrasting smooth skin song the rest of Eden's curves. And she did have curves. Asha shook herself, remembering Eden's comment about desires. How many came to save the princess only to want to destroy or devour her? To own her. Asha's own blood heats at the thought in anger. Eden steps down from the bed and grabs a silky robe hanging on a hook on the wall. Smoothly, she slides into it. It must have slits for her wings as they do not cause the fabric to bunch or get caught. She returns and walks to Asha, still splayed out on the ground. The robe skims the tops of her thighs, the hemline singed black. She stands before Asha and tilts her head to one side and lifts a solitary brow.

"You said you had questions. Do you intend to ask them from the floor?" Asha feels heat run to her cheeks.

"No. Of course not." She scrambles up and finds herself now standing on even footing with Eden. Shockingly, the powerful woman is shorter than her by a good few inches, though Asha's own boots do give her a bit of a lift. It is clear the woman was petite...long hair sweeping over her breasts down to the middle of her waist. But Asha was actively telling her mind not to acknowledge that part. She looked around her but there was no other furniture in the space but the large four poster.

"Um, should we just..." Eden gave her a smirk.

"Yes, I am rather lacking in furniture." Eden walks over to the fireplace. Logs are stacked beside it. She adds a few to the hearth and then as if in slow motion she breathes almost seductively over the wood. As she stands back, a flame grows in front of her. Eden turns back to face Asha, a silhouette in the light of the fire she literally breathed to life. Asha swallows reflexively. She was definitely going to be turning on this woman's spit over the flames of hell, and she might even thank her for it.

"I'm not picky. Thank you." Asha says and on still trembling legs she makes her way to the hearth and both women settle on a rather comfortable rug stained with soot before it.

Asha takes a deep breath and lets it out slowly.

"So, I feel like the first question is an obvious one..." Asha says as her eyes move from Eden's expectant face to the wings settled nicely behind her as she sits.

Eden hummed for a moment.

"I was cursed." Eden answers.

"Cursed?" Asha asks gently, prompting. Eden nods. She stares into the fire, getting lost in her own head it seemed.

"It wasn't supposed to be a curse, not really. But magic is complicated and if messed with or performed by those who are more cruel than they seem...well." Eden shrugs, letting her wings flutter behind her.

"So it wasn't you who sought out magic?" Asha asks. Eden shakes her head.

"My parents, once the king and queen of this castle, sought to protect me and put their trust in the wrong person." Eden's voice sank at the memory of her parents.

"But no one has been king or queen of this kingdom, from this castle in hundreds of years!" Ash blurts out in disbelief.

Eden smirks sadly.

"Eight hundred and forty-seven years, to be exact. Since my parents perished."

"But that would make you..."

"Yes," Eden sighs, a touch exasperated, her head tips back, exposing the column of her throat.

"I'm almost 1,000 years old, give or take a lifetime."

"I'm sorry?" Asha mumbles looking down. And she was. She hated being alone. Had never been alone in the apartments she had shared with her dads and eight siblings. She couldn't imagine Eden's plight. She did, illuminated just now by the flickering firelight, look just incredibly sad to Asha.

"Then why kill everyone who has come to this castle to save you?" Asha asks, aware this could be the question that ends the conversation and starts dinner.

Eden leans back on her palms and lets her head roll so she can look at Asha. Asha feels as though a trail of heat follows Eden's gaze, leaving her mouth dry and her pants decidedly not. Eden's nostrils flare and she closes her eyes.

"My parents' idea was to protect me from those who have

impure desires for my crown. The spell made it so every urge of those around me was amplified, almost irresistible to act upon. Some I let go, long ago. Others were so driven by that feeling I kindled in them that after release they returned, usually with chains sometimes with armies."

"They returned?" Asha managed to ask, the heat in her core building despite her best efforts to watch Eden's face and not the flow of silk over small breasts. She had the presence of mind to try to control her breathing as her core clenched on nothing and she felt the brush of her own breast bindings harden her nipples.

"They wanted to own me, my body, one way or another. It was harder to subdue them when they didn't come back alone. They would stop at nothing, killed everyone who could resist and be near me. So, I stopped letting them go." Her voice was calm, matter of fact. Asha shook her head.

"And you can't control this?" She asks, trying to keep her voice even.

Eden opens one burning amber eye that had fallen closed as she reminisced and smiled.

"Oh, I can, to an extent. The pull on your desires is always evident when you are around me, but I can, with focus increase its intensity."

"And," Asha gulped against a dry throat, "are you doing that now?" Asha blinks, realizing she was leaning forward, and Eden had moved to mirror her.

Eden's nostrils flared again. Her amber eyes dilated until her irises were only a thin ring of fire around her pupils. She releases a sigh.

"It is so rare I get to play with my food." Eden breathes onto Asha's ear, punctuating her statement with a nip to Asha's earlobe.

Asha couldn't hold back the whine the action pulled from

her. Her eyes flutter shut as Eden's clawed hand lands on her shoulder and slides over her neck, letting the tips of her claws lightly scratch then dig in just so as she tips Asha's face up by her chin.

Eden didn't shy away. Her lips press in hard and demanding on Asha's own. Asha didn't know if it was the little bite Eden gave the corner of her mouth with her fanged canines or if Eden amped up her pervasive powers that caused Asha's panties to flood.

Asha moaned her permission letting Eden's tongue dart into her mouth, kitten licks teasing her tongue. Asha was sure she would have fallen over. She was leaning so hard towards Eden, if Eden's own hands, exploring her back and arms weren't keeping her upright.

One of Eden's hands squeezes Asha's biceps as the other tangles in her cropped hair and pulls.

Eden pushed Asha away. Asha lets out an embarrassing whine. Eden chuckles.

"I can hold my breath a lot longer than you. You need to breathe, Asha." She explains, a rough gravelly tone having entered her voice. Asha realizes she's right and gasps for air, being held up by the toned arm of the dragoness before her. As she sucks in air Eden's head cocks to the side, causing the shoulder of her silk robe to slip off her shoulder, revealing the swell of her breast.

"You are wearing entirely too much, don't you agree, Asha?" She says as she lets a single clawed finger skate from the nape of Asha's neck to her collarbone until coming to a rest on the collar of her shirt. Asha gives a breathy nod. Eden's answering smile is deadly. The nail slices through the woven fabric of the shirt and continues through Asha's breast bindings like butter. The fabric and wrappings fall open and off at the simple ministrations of Eden's claws. Carefully, Eden trails her fingers down until she can cup one breast in her palm. Gently, she massages. Asha moans and is met with a small hum from Eden. Eden licks her lips.

"Delicious." She purrs. And that was the only warning Asha gets before Eden's lips begin to paint her with blooms of heat with every touch of her lips.

Eden begins along the slope of Asha's jaw, planting featherlight kisses until she travels down the length of her throat.

"Right here I can hear your pulse, the way it quickens whenever I touch you somewhere new. I wonder what it will do when I do this." Eden whispers before scraping her fangs along the pulse in Asha's neck. Asha gasps, her hand coming up to cradle Eden's head in response. She nudges Eden's mouth closer, tips her head back farther and pants as she looks up to the ash coated ceiling. Eden chuckles, sending goosebumps along Asha's arms, and bites down, suckling at the skin, bringing the blood to the surface.

"Eden!" Asha can't help but shout. Before Asha can catch her wits, Eden pulls back and without even admiring her handiwork of what Asha is sure must be a masterpiece of a love bite Eden continues down, licking a long stripe down her chest until she holds Asha's breath aloft. She pulls back and from under hooded eyes and blushing cheeks she meet's Asha's panting gaze. She holds eye contact with Asha as she leans down and blows a warm breath over her nipple, causing it to pebble and Asha to whine. She realizes she still has her hands on Eden's head and pulls the red head closer. Eden opens her mouth and pulls Asha's breast into her mouth. Her tongue flicks at her nipple as she sucks it between her teeth. Asha feels her knees shake where she kneels. Eden's hand caresses from Asha's shoulder, trailing along until she grabs her hand. She takes it and pulls it towards her chest. Her skin is smooth and Eden's nipple pebbles against her palm. The dragoness moans around her nipple and leans into her hand. Asha's breath catches, but she manages to knead the gorgeous woman torturing her breast.

"Eden...I need..." Asha moans shamelessly. Either by her ministrations or by her powers Asha is beyond able to fight her burning want for this woman in front of her. She rubs her thighs together where she sits, aching for relief and unable to garner any as she feels as though she burns alive.

"I know," Eden giggles then, "and oh, so do I. Isn't that marvelous?" Eden says, letting go of Asha's nipple with a pop and shimmying to relieve herself of the rest of her robe. Asha watches her lean into her palm and cautiously brings up another. She is becoming aware of another need rising inside her. Not only does she want to be taken by Eden, utterly and completely she wants to make Eden feel the same desire, the same frenzy and hopefully release that Asha was chasing.

As Asha contemplates this, she leans forward and recaptures Eden's lips. Her other hand begins to explore. She begins by cupping Eden's sharp cheekbones, turning her face to accommodate their kiss as it turns sloppier with Eden opening her mouth and letting Asha explore her teeth and tongue. Asha's hand then runs down and over one shoulder towards Eden's back. She lets it drift, feeling along warm smooth skin as she approaches where skin turns to scale, human flesh to dragon's wing. Her fingertips skate along the space where one wing meets skin causing them to flare out just slightly making Asha grip the scales between the where the wing disappear into Eden's back in order to keep Eden from inadvertently pulling away from their kiss due to the wings' opening. Despite this effort, the kiss is broken anyway as Eden pulls away and bends, pushing her forehead into the crux of Asha's neck and shoulder. Eden moans.

"Oh." She says when Asha stills, holding the dragoness and not moving any further.

"Oh?" she croaks. From the cradle of her neck, Eden nods slightly, adjusting to nip at Asha's protruding collarbone.

"Do that again." Eden orders and Asha is helpless but to comply. Gently but with intention she digs into the space between Eden's wings, applying steady pressure. The lips that had been busy at the juncture of her neck and shoulders stutter as another guttural moan is released followed by a whine when Asha stops again.

"You really like that," Asha states in amazement. Eden pulls her head up. Her red hair has flown about her face as she pants. Asha is mesmerized.

"You need to take your damned pants off Asha." Eden finally rasps when she's seemed to catch her breath. Asha nods earnestly and Eden wastes no time reaching down to the ties at her pants and gets frustrated with the knot. She looses a growl and with a swipe of her claws cuts the laces. Asha smirks and lets her own nails lightly scrape down the center of Eden's back along the scales. Eden's back bows and she whines. Asha chuckles.

Eden pants and makes quick eye contact before capturing Asha's mouth once again. This time both their hands explore, grabbing, kneading, and when Eden breaks contact to let Asha gasp for air once again, she uses her considerable upper arm strength to gently lay Asha down upon the rug in front of the hearth. Asha hums with delight as the dragoness continues her exploration down Asha's body. She doesn't stay long on her collarbone this time. Her tongue traces a path down as Eden's claws make quick work of what's left of Asha's shirt. It falls beside Asha as once again her nipple is taken into the hot, wet mouth of Eden.

As Eden's teeth tease and scrape to the underside of one

breast, her hands gently cup and squeeze the other. It is taking entirely too long for Asha.

"Eden...." She whines. Eden pops off her breast with a wicked grin and shushes her with one finger to Asha's lips.

"Patience." She croons with a crooked brow. Eden waits until Asha nods shakily, the desire still thrumming through her blood. Eden returns to her mission. She blows a breath of hot air over the nipple she had rolled between her thumb and fore-finger, keeping eye contact the entire time. Asha holds still and tries unsuccessfully to swallow another moan.

"Good girl." She purrs. And Asha gasps, aware the phrase was just absolutely ruined for her now. Eden kitten licks the nipple before her but doesn't stay long. Asha doesn't know if she should apologize, beg her to go back, continue the sweet torture. BUt Eden continues kissing her way down Asha's abdomen until stopped by the ruined pants, laces cut to mere ribbons.

Eden raises a singular claw and applies pressure upon the worn but heavy cloth that makes up Asha's pants. The pressure allows for the claw to rip the crotch of her pants down the seam as well as to provide a featherlight feeling over where Asha really needs Eden. Asha continues to make no complaint as Eden quickly tears the fabric off her legs, leaving Asha bare to the dragoness.

"Much better don't you think?" Eden says. Her wings are flared slightly and Asha answers with a scratch along Eden's scaled spine where she can still reach. Eden's eyelashes flutter, but her eyes do not close.

"So needy." She teases instead, and Eden feels her heart rate climb even more if that's possible as Eden lowers her head.

"Eden, please." She manages as the redhead hovers over Asha's dripping core. Her clit is swollen with need, peeking from its hood. She's almost sure the same featherlight touch from before will send Asha over the edge she's been flirting with since those claws first began to demolish her only clothes. Eden smiles calmly, serenely.

Asha watches her upper body lower until Eden's mouth sits criminally close to Asha's pussy. The dragoness inhales and moans. Her mouth opens and bites a bit roughly into the flesh of Asha's inner thigh, causing her to shout. However, the pain of the powerful canines only causes Asha to gush more.

"I apologize, but you smell divine, and I couldn't help myself." Eden sounds delirious. Asha pants and licks her lips, trying to find her voice again.

"Eden, if you don't eat my pussy in the next ten seconds..." Asha's empty threat is cut off by the swipe of a criminally long tongue through her folds past her entrance before flicking her clit. Asha chokes on a small scream.

"Be careful what you ask for, Asha." Eden chuckles and before Asha can beg, pray for the return of the sensation, Eden's tongue dives back down. The tip swirls over Asha's clit, highly sensitive from the hours? Minutes? Eons? Of teasing and magic pheromones, of foreplay between the two women. Eden lifts both of Asha's legs with her clawed strong hands and situates them over her shoulders to give her better leverage to dive into Asha's sex. Her tongue explores her folds and licks up every drop of Asha's wetness. Periodically, the tip returns to flick at her clit, sending spears of fire to her core. Asha pants above the dragoness and feels herself edging ever closer.

"Eden!" she warns. The dragoness removes her tongue from the enlarged clit and almost lazily returns to licking her way from the top of Asha's sex to her entrance. Then, finally, without further warning Eden's tongue plunges inside Asha. Asha looses a scream that would rattle window frames if there were any in this castle tower. It hadn't clicked until then, the other physical enhancement from Eden's dragon curse. A tongue almost twice the length of any Asha had seen was buried deep inside her, exploring her walls, curling to press into the spot on her inner walls that would drive her feral. Asha bow bends as the assault is not just inside her but continued on her clit by the rhythmic circling of the pad of Eden's finger. Asha's heels dig into the small of Eden's back, over the last of her scales at the base of her spine before skin curves over a voluptuous ass.

The action caused the dragoness to moan into Asha's pussy and she redoubled her efforts, tongue diving deeper while her finger relentlessly applied pressure to Asha's clit. And there it was, the edging leading to sweet release. Asha's panting lost its rhythm and she keened.

"Eden. Eden. Eden I'm." Asha tried to warn the magnificent woman, but her release hit her system. It started as a bright burning crescendo at her center, sending licks of fire and lightning up her spine through her skin and to each hair follicle. Asha knows she must have screamed. Knows if anyone was outside the tower, they'd assume she was in fact just consumed by the dragon lurking in the castle's walls. And oh, how right they were.

Asha comes back to her body to the gentle sensation of small licks around her walls. A soft, almost soothing rhythm of slight pressure on her clit working her through her aftershocks. Asha managed to leverage herself onto her elbows to look down at Eden.

Eden's eyes flick up to meet her own. The woman looks incredibly satisfied with herself. Her wings sway lazily on her back over Asha's legs and Eden pillowed her cheek on one of Asha's thighs. Asha could feel how she still shuddered against her. Eden had devoured Asha, but was now on the precipice of her own torture. Asha removed her legs, thigh burning with the effort, from over Eden's shoulders. She sat up and cupped one of Eden's cheeks, giving the princess her own cheesy soft smile.

"Eden, I would very much like to return the favor. Do you want me to?" Asha asks, her voice barely audible, completely raw from moaning and screaming. But she wanted Eden to know she had a choice, and she could act on it, on her own desires instead of fighting off other people's demands as she had done for almost 1,000 years. Asha reaches up with one hand and caresses the red wavy locks mussed from the vigorous activities they'd just done.

Eden blinks at her and Asha sees tears begin to well in her eyes.

"I will not judge you for wanting, for letting me give you what you want. I will also, despite the mind-blowing orgasm you just gave me, never demand I have the right to touch you the same way."

Asha could still feel the need, feel the want to have her lips paint constellations across the unmarred map of Eden's body. She also feels a deep protectiveness, a desire to keep her happy and safe and cared for. She wonders if it was the sad, faraway pain in Eden's eyes that hid under her overconfident and untouchable veneer or the mind-blowing sex that made the needs reset. She knew the effect Eden's own powers could be having, escalating her own desires. But Asha was strong and though she had succumbed to her own sexual mind melting need, it was with consent, with the coupled desire of Eden's choice to devour her as well. So, she no longer feels that it was unbearable, she can and would bear it. She hopes the dragoness doesn't desire to truly eat her anymore. Though some deep-rooted instinct knows she is safe in the dragoness' arms now. And though she would love, wildly, to be eaten again she doesn't fear for her life in Eden's hands. She watches Eden as she seems to weigh Asha's words in her head. Finally, she gives a small nod.

"I need you to tell me, Princess." Asha says quietly. Eden swallows.

"I need you, Asha, please." Eden's voice is smaller than it had been all night and the please tacked onto the end of her sentence makes another coil of desire begin in her stomach.

"Then, for you, we will do this properly." Asha says determined. She stands and pulls the dragoness to her feet. They are surrounded by Eden's robe, the remains of Asha's clothes, and the embers of the dying fire. Almost all Asha can see by is the light of the moon once more and the dragon princess' glowing amber eyes.

Asha leads Eden by one hand back to her four-poster bed. Both women are quiet as Asha gently pulls Eden to the sheets.

"Lie down." Asha says softly. Eden complies, falling back onto the sheets, red hair pooling around her. Almost naturally, her legs fall open and in the moonlight, Asha can see her folds glistening.

Asha climbs onto the bed and situates herself above her on all fours.

"If you ever want to stop, just tell me." She whispers, eyes lidded before leaning down and recapturing the woman's lips. They are swollen and soft from their ministrations. Asha explores Eden's mouth slowly as she lets the rest of her body lie slowly on top of Eden. Asha makes sure to lie just so her thigh meets Eden's core. And when it does a soft whimper escapes the terrifying woman who clutches at Asha's arms, trying very hard not to scratch her with her claws.

As Asha begins to rock her leg up into Eden's core, she pulls back from the kiss, biting her lower lip and letting it pull as scrapes her teeth along it.

"Does this feel good?" Asha asks, accompanying the

rocking of her hips with one hand that she had slid between Eden's body and the bed digging a bit into her scales. They are smooth and layered and when she rustles them a whole-body shiver assaults Eden.

"Oh Asha," Eden's eyes roll back in her head, and she seems torn between rocking up into her thigh or grinding her body back down onto her fingers. "Yes, very good." She manages finally.

"Good." Asha says and allows herself something she had wanted since before Eden had slipped into the discarded silk robe. She takes one perfect rose bud nipple into her mouth and lightly sucks at it in her mouth. Eden moans shamelessly and one hand comes up, grabbing her hair, tugging slightly on Asha's hair but pushing her mouth harder against her breast. Asha moans, sending vibrations over Eden's nipple and the dragoness whimpers.

"Asha... need...something...please." The dragoness is worked up and practically writhes under Asha on the bed.

Asha removes her hand from under Eden's back, causing the woman to whine, missing the steady pressure on the sensitive scales. Asha pops off the breast she was worshiping and shushes Eden.

"Don't worry, I've got you." Eden says and groans a bit as she feels the slick on her thigh. Eden is so wet Asha practically glides over her folds. She knows Eden won't last long, her desire building as she ate Asha out on the floor just minutes ago. Asha moves back down to the breasts that have captured her attention. She licks open mouthed at the nipple sitting pebbled but as of yet untouched before her. As she does this, she slides her now unoccupied hand between her thigh and Eden's wet pussy.

Eden moans as Asha gathers wetness from Eden's entrance and begins to circle her clit, red and throbbing. Eden's hips jerk beneath her, and Asha knows she is getting close already. Asha swirls her fingers around Eden's clit one more time before gathering wetness on her fingers and letting one finger slip into the ready heat of Eden's pussy. She immediately is sucked in by the eager woman's sex and Asha crooks a finger. The action causes Eden's back to bow, thrusting her breast more into Asha's mouth as her wings extend with a snap against the sheet.

"Again." Eden demands, "Asha, please do that again." And well, Asha is helpless to comply. She crooks her finger inside Eden, rubbing against the spot she knows she will find on her inner walls. Eden has seemed to lose control and thrashes her head from side to side, eyes closed shut.

"I'm..." Eden pants and lets out a small whine. "I need..."

And Asha doesn't need any more instruction than that. She pulls out her finger from the delicious heat and thrusts back in with two, curling them in the way she had learned is just right. She pulls away from where she has littered Eden's chest with love bites and focuses on her efforts as she speeds up her thrusts. Eden meeting her thrusts, lost to the delirium of a rising orgasm. Asha can see it though. She needs one last push. She leans forward, placing her mouth next to Eden's ear.

"It's alright Eden. Take it. Take what you need." And the acknowledgement is all Eden needs to let go. Her orgasm rocks through her, her walls lamping down hard on Asha's fingers who rocks her hand to work her through the spasms.

She watches the princess come down. First her wings settle, relaxed from their strained position, then her back sinks into the mattress, and finally her thighs and walls release her. Eden's eyes flutter open to mere slits. Asha watches her as she slowly and gently removes her fingers from Eden's pussy, bringing them up to her mouth. She holds eye contact as she licks off every drop. Eden pants beneath her.

Once she seems to catch her breath, Asha moves to lay beside the princess. Eden follows her with her eyes.

"That was..." she says and simply ends the thought with a sigh. Asha smiles, happy with her performance and feeling the coil of her desire begin to burn once more.

"I'm glad." She says instead, not wanting to rush or pressure the beautiful creature before her into anything more than she was willing to do, willing to give. She watches however, as the dragoness' nostrils flare as they look at each other. Asha realizes that just as before the woman can smell her arousal rising. Asha blushes and Eden smiles.

"You're insatiable, aren't you?" Eden inquires, correctly guessing that Asha has several more rounds in her. Eden chuckles and pushes her upper body up onto one forearm. As she does, the jewel necklace that has continued to adorn the hollow of her throat glints in the moonlight, shifting as the chain snaps and the necklace delicately falls to the few inches of sheets between the women.

Eden gasps and stares at the necklace she last saw off her neck as a young girl. Asha's eyes widened.

"Did...did that just happen?" She whispers. Her eyes quickly track over behind Eden's shoulders. The wings, now held tight to Eden's body with stress, are still there as are the scales and her claws and amber eyes. Eden blinks, seeming to try to understand. She looks up to Asha then.

"I suppose that is one way to end a curse." Asha raises a brow at the princess.

"You are still a dragon. But the necklace broke. But I didn't have pure intentions. I wanted you, I was desperate for you to take me, I don't..." Eden shushes her with a passionate kiss. Asha really is helpless but to comply. Eden pulls back and her smile is radiant.

"I don't think it was about you resisting your desires or

having only pure desires as my parents wished." Eden says, her voice bewildered, as if she is thinking out loud.

"What then?" Asha asks exasperated.

"You gave me the license to follow my desires, whatever they may have been. Even when you desperately wanted a certain outcome, you knew the decision was mine." She says, her voice heavy as her eyes get wet. Asha's eyes widen and she caresses the redhead before her. She leans in and gives her a small peck on the nose, then she takes a breath.

"That is called consent, and it is the most bullshit thing I have ever heard. That's what breaks the curse? Allowing you to have agency as a woman in power over yourself, your body, fuck your queendom! How in the world did that take almost one thousand..." But Asha's tirade is cut off by open mouth laughing kisses from the dragon princess. Asha allows it and wraps her arms around this new, wonderful treasure that's fallen into her lap.

And Asha is right. Their night is long. The women talk and they don't. They decide to show Eden the world. And when faced with the pesky little problem of the King who hired Asha, he receives the world's most ridiculous red jewel necklace with a note that wishes him the best of luck with the magic to teach him how to woo a bride.

And Asha and Eden, well after Asha descends the tower in an ash-stained sheet, they find proper clothes and live a proper life. Their life.

ABOUT THE AUTHOR

Alyson Tong writes sapphic romance, fantasy, and historical fiction. She writes for adults and YA. She is working on her first children's books as well. She loves anime and Disney and her English Bulldog Goose, oh and her wife as well. They all live together in the SF East Bay, where Alyson works as a teacher and finds time to scribble scenes between singing nursery rhymes to two-year-olds in her preschool class. Check her out online on Instagram, TikTok and Twitter.

- Instagram: https://www.instagram.com/alysonrtongwrites/

- TikTok: https://www.tiktok.com/@thenerdiestofalys

- Twitter: https://twitter.com/nerdiestofalys

AFTERWORD

When authors get in groups and talk about author things online, where their (often) introverted selves can hide behind a keyboard, cool things can happen. Many months ago, I had a brainstorm to have a bunch of authors put some of the hottest scenes in their books—with some of their most beloved characters—into a collection for sale, 'Sapphic Sizzle.'

Lots of authors thought that was a great idea. A couple of dozen stepped forward. Scenes started getting submitted. A few weeks in, the gnashing of the teeth began.

Many of the indie authors who wanted to participate have their books exclusively with one major online retailer, yours truly included. There are many and varied reasons why authors do this—mine is a lack of time—but, by so doing, they're bound by certain terms. Only so much of a book can be repeated elsewhere. You can't sell a book with an excerpt from an exclusive book on another retail site and so forth. The project was scrapped. Sort of.

The 'Sapphic Sizzle' idea was re-born as a collection of all original short stories. A dozen plus authors signed on, all indie or hybrid. We lost a few along the way, but we completed this book with ten authors. A few used familiar characters. A few used characters we're just getting to know in oh so intimate ways.

Some of these stories are smoky. Some truly sizzle. All come from the pens and keyboards of some wonderful people I'm happy to call friends. They come from around the world, too: Canada, Columbia, around the US, around the UK and more before they got where they are now.

We hope you enjoyed these stories. Thank you for buying or for borrowing this book. Thank you for supporting indie authors, and thank you most of all for supporting Sapphic fiction.